MY BOYFRIEND'S WIFE 2
Make The Pain Stop

Mychea

Good 2 Go Publishing

ISBN: 9781943686766
Copyright ©2016
Published 2016 by Good2Go Publishing
7311 W. Glass Lane • Laveen, AZ 85339
www.good2gopublishing.com
twitter @good2gobooks
G2G@good2gopublishing.com
Facebook.com/good2gopublishing
ThirdLane Marketing: Brian James
Brian@good2gopublishing.com
Cover design: Davida Baldwin
Interior Layout: Mychea, Inc

Printed in the U.S.A.

Books By This Author

Coveted

Vengeance

Omega *(Coming Soon)*

He Loves Me, He Loves You Not

He Loves Me, He Loves You Not 2

He Loves Me, He Loves You Not 3

He Loves Me, He Loves You Not 4

He Loves Me, He Loves You Not 5

My Boyfriend's Wife

My Boyfriend's Wife 2

U Promised Part 1 *(e-book short)*

U Promised Part 2 *(e-book short coming soon)*

DVD

My Boyfriend's Wife Stage Play

Acknowledgments •••

Thank you to all of my amazing readers.

You're the reason that I keep knocking out these novels.

Enjoy!

Recap • • •

Hunter sat on the bench near Ananda's grave holding tight to Maddox and Ariane as each sat on his knees, little hands cuddling the teddy bears their mother had given them on their birthday with Caprice and Tatiana looking on. With a lump the size of a lemon in his throat, he fought back the only tears he had shed since Ananda's death. In less than three years, he had made her into an international superstar and in a matter of seconds, she had been taken from the industry, her son and daughter, and the world. "Ready to go?" Lorna asked him softly as she walked up and gently took Maddox thus freeing him up to carry Ariane. "Yeah, there's nothing more we can do here," he said sadly as the six of them made their way to the waiting car and away from Ananda's final resting place.

MY BOYFRIEND'S WIFE 2

Make The Pain Stop

Prologue • • •

"I want a divorce," Nikki announced, as she walked into the room that her husband occupied.

Theodore looked up from his notes staring at his wife wondering what had gotten into her.

"Did you hear what I said? I want a divorce." Nikki emphasized every word so that he would get the point.

"I heard you loud and clear." Theodore began slowly, "What I fail to understand is why you want a divorce? Everything is good, we haven't had any problems, what's going on with you?" he inquired genuinely surprised by her request. He was under the impression that he and Nikki had a good marriage. Of course they argued here and there, but for the most part their relationship was solid gold. Or so he had thought.

"I've been seeing someone." Nikki informed him matter-of-factly.

Theodore pushed the papers he had been reviewing to the side of the dining room table that he had been going over for a recent interview he had conducted and just stared at Nikki as if she had lost her mind. Wondering what had brought on this current situation and marveling at her boldness to just announce it like that.

Nikki was his wife of eight years. They had two sons together and this was the first he had heard anything of a divorce. He prided himself on being one of the few males that he knew who didn't cheat on his wife so he couldn't understand why she had it in her mind that she was going to divorce him and had the nerve to sit here very confidently stating that she had been seeing someone else.

The two of them met in college. They had both been on the Debate Team and one thing he had always respected about Nikki was her mind. She'd graduated with a 4.5 GPA. Her mind was what had made her incredibly attractive to him. Her looks hadn't hurt either. His wife was a deep cocoa brown with dark brown eyes that slanted just a little at the corners. Her hair reminded him of soft cotton when he touched it. It was a beautiful mass of black curls that she kept short. She was 5'7, a petite size 2 and after two babies, still sexy as hell.

"When did this happen?"

She shrugged indifferently. "One of those times that you were on the road. Why does it matter? It's done. I moved on and I want out."

Theodore stood up and began approaching her slowly.

"So you're just willing to walk away from our marriage and our history just like that?"

"I'm not talking about anything. You're never home. I always have the boys by myself. We have sex maybe once a month. That does not make a marriage, she pointed out to him. "I need someone who's in a relationship with me and I have found that elsewhere. I just need to know if you're going to make this divorce easy or difficult."

"So that's it, huh? Your mind is already made up? No talking about this? No going to counseling? Just boom, you out?" Theodore clapped his hands together.

"Yeah, I'm not really one for counseling." Nikki scrunched up her face. "You know me I go with the flow. I think it and go with it. I stick with my decisions. It is what it is," she told him with no hint of love or remorse left in her voice.

"Let's at least go to counseling before we make any final decisions." Theodore told her. "What about the boys did you think about them before you made this hasty decision?"

"The boys will be fine," Nikki told him. "I'm not really trying to alter their life. That's why we're going to stay here in the brownstone and you're going to find a new apartment."

Theodore's calm demeanor suddenly went into a rage. He was angry that she had already thought this completely through and made decisions on his behalf without even consulting him first.

"So you think you just going to kick me out of my house? Is that what this is?" he demanded to know.

"It's not just your house. It is our house and the only reason I'm making this decision is not to alter the boy's lifestyle that much. At the end of the day, I think they deserve to come home to the same house they've been coming home to all this time. It's only fair," Nikki told him.

"Oh, fair for them." Teddy replied sarcastically. "But forget about good old Ted, huh? Just he gonna be alright, huh? You know this really is some basic shit. You new millennium women kill me with this dumb stuff. You actually got a man holding you down and you pull this stunt?"

Nikki knew that he was highly upset because Teddy was not the cursing type. It just wasn't his style.

"Look. I'm not trying to set some millennial record or what not. I'm just trying to let you know what's going on and what the situation is going to be. This is where we are at this point and I really don't see anything else that can be done here. I'm done with this relationship. I've done all I can do here and I want out."

Teddy was seeing red. It was taking everything inside of him not to lash out at her. This is what the good guys had to endure. He knew so many guys running around here being Dogs and yet their women were loyal to them. He was loyal to his woman and she was out being a dog treating him as if he was nothing more than some poo she has stepped in from outside.

"I refuse to be disrespected in my house."

"Our house," Nikki corrected him.

"Whatever, maybe I'm not dealing with you today. You can take your new man and you want to be divorced ass up out of my face. Let a new man deal with your drama because you do have plenty. I've dealt with a lot with you through the years and I stayed because I love you and you were my college sweetheart but if you can't respect me and our marriage then that's fine but I'm not giving up my house."

"Look your words don't mean anything to me honey," Nikki said shaking her head. "You're not staying in the house. Let's be clear. The boys and I are going to stay here. I am NOT their life do you understand? I would hate to have to call the police and report a domestic dispute. Do you understand where I'm going with this?"

Theodore just shook his head. "You are so far. You know what? Keep the house, keep everything in it. I just want to be away from you. I'm done." Grabbing his notes off the table, he put everything into his workbag and left the house.

"You always knew Nikki was crazy," Matt said later that day when Theodore chose to stay with him for the night.

"Thanks for letting me crash here until I find something."

"Anytime. You know you always got some-where to stay as long as I'm breathing breath in my lungs. I'm just trying to figure out what came over your shorty."

"You and me both. I guess a new dick in the picture with do that to anybody."

"Yeah but you better hope your new man don't get her ass fired. Because she can be pretty difficult from what I remember. I told you not to marry that girl." Matthew reminded him.

"That you did. Mad that you did but I wouldn't trade it for the world. I loved her in college and I love her now. She's the mother of my children and we are going to figure out this co-parenting thing for the sake of the boys otherwise she would most definitely have to watch your back."

"Here, here brother. Here, here, Matthew said after clinking their beer mugs together.

The wounded, the heartless and the undeserving;

hide behind charisma, false promises and sincerity

That's how the good and deserving

get caught up in the mix

Believing the lies as truth; the façade

Victim of the game...or willing participant

So many questions, not enough answers

The game; pressure of continuing wrong

When you now know right

The suffering involved

Make the pain stop...

I think that men are the scum of the freakin' earth. Yeah, I said it...so? What you gonna do about it? My reasons are valid and while I speak in general terms because they aren't all bad, most of them aren't all good either. The games they play. The women they hurt. Selfish they are, but happy. I guess I'd be happy to if I took a note from their book and had one man at home paying bills, then had another one somewhere else that I hung out with for fun, then had the other one for the great sex. You know, something like a line up. But I'm not built like that. I have feelings and a heart to say the least. Am I a victim? No. After I found out about the situation, I became a willing participant because I didn't leave and that makes me part to blame.

But you know what kills me? It doesn't matter what you look like. You can be petite, a perfect size four, long hair, tan skin, weigh one hundred and twenty pounds with curves like me and they will still dog you out. But that's neither here nor there. Let me keep it moving along.

So, I won't subject you to my woe is me story. Just facts, at first I didn't know and it was all good. Then I did know and it went all bad. Feel me? Okay, I've talked your head off long enough. Let's get this charade started. I was going to say let the games begin, because it all seems to be games. However, this time I will just throw it out there, let's get to the drama. That's how you like it and that's how I'm beginning to understand it to be.

~ The unamused...

Chase

Chapter 1

● ● ●

"Here comes the tyrant now. Make sure you have her coffee ready."

"I have it right here. Nice and hot for her."

"Good. I'd hate to be you otherwise."

Chase brushed past her two assistants without a word of greeting. Her mind was in another place. Shutting the opulent mahogany door with a loud slam, she willed her body to stop shaking.

Chase's phone rang.

"Hello."

"It's your dad."

"Mom?" Chase was bewildered. Her mother never called her and that was not an exaggeration.

"Yes baby," her mom continued. "Your dad. Your dad he, he didn't wake up this morning."

"What?" Her brain was trying to comprehend what was going on. "Are you telling me that Daddy passed away?"

"Yes. That's exactly what I'm trying to say," her mother told her on the other end of the line.

"I'm so sorry baby he's gone."

"Thank you for letting me know," Chase responded calmly as she hung up the phone.

Pushing the intercom button on the phone in her office she quickly. Extension 643.

"It's about time you came in. You're never late. What's going on?" The lightly tinged Puerto Rican New York accent serenaded her from the speakerphone.

"Please come into my office," Chase responded before disconnecting the call.

"What's wrong?" Marcie asked as she came flying through the door.

She smiled in spite of her current mood as her best friend. Marcie rushed into her office in less than a minute flat. Considering she was on the sixth floor and Chase is on the twelfth Chase had to wonder if she had teleportation powers that she had never claimed.

"It's that no good Anthony isn't it?" Marcie shook her head. "I know an asshole when I see one. I never liked him."

Chase stared at Marcie as she paced the floor having yet to respond.

"You know I could take him out. I've fought men before. I'm down."

A solitary tear slid down Chase's face. *What is this tear about?* Chase wondered.

"My mother called to tell me that my dad passed away this morning."

Marcie's eyes grew about four inches their normal size. "Oh my gosh, are you okay?"

Marcie raced to her side. "I am such an idiot." She pulled Chase in her arms. "I'm so sorry Cha Cha. What happened to him?"

Wrapping her arms around Marcie, Chase returned the hug and lay her head on her friend's shoulder.

"Mommy said he just didn't wake up this morning. She said last night he came home, had his dinner, and went to bed like normal. Then this morning she tried waking him up for breakfast and he wasn't there. He must have passed away sometime during the night."

"Oh, you poor baby." Trying to console her friend Marcie continued, "Why did you come into the office today?"

"Because my job is my everything. I need to focus on something other than my dad right now," Chase continued, pulling out of Marcie's arms.

"You sure that you're okay?"

"Yes, I'm fine. I'm fine. Now back to this whole job thing. I think I need a break," Chase told Marcie indifferently. "I'm tired of writing," she continued.

"Why do you say that? You're doing so well at it," Marcie said to her.

"Yeah, but my heart just isn't into it anymore."

"I'm sorry to hear that." Marcie looked at Chase sympathetically. She wondered why she felt that way because right now Chase was at the top of her game. The literary world had finally come knocking. Her New York Times best-selling novel was about to be turned into a movie and things were going great. As her agent and best friend, Marcie wasn't exactly sure how to feel about this new turn of events.

"It's just that I'm bored," Chase said looking at her wondering how she was taking the news.

"So are you telling me that you want to maybe try another genre?"

"I'm just saying I really don't know what I want to do right now." Chase shrugged. "I feel like I just need to live a little, you know. I've spent years trying to get here and now that I'm here living in my moment, I just don't know if I want to do it anymore. The thrill is gone so to speak."

"Okay, well as your agent I am a little confused. We have so many deals in place, we really can't afford for you not to be a part of what's going on right now. However, as your friend, one of your best friends, may I add, I feel as if you should take this time to explore what it is you want to do career wise. What goals you may have and what you want to do with the rest of your life," Marcie told her.

"Right now I just want to focus on me. I don't know what's going on with my career. But I need time to figure it all out and examine exactly what it is that I'm trying to do it myself."

"What you don't really have is enough time for that. We have so many obligations that you've already signed contracts for and you cannot back out. You just can't," Marcie emphasized. "We have things we have to do Chase and I really need you to jump on board here."

Chase cut her eyes at Marcie. She loved that her best friend was her agent but right now, she just wasn't in the mood to deal with her persistence. "I am definitely on board Marcie. I just, I'm not going to not do my job. But I just need a moment."

"A moment you don't have. But after all of these current obligations are out of the way, we will definitely schedule you some down time. I guarantee it."

"Thanks, that will be much appreciated," Chase told her.

****

"Okay, so here's the deal. I've decided that I'm going to see other women. Actually, that's inaccurate. I'm already seeing another woman."

Chase stared at her phone imagining it to be Anthony's face. "I'm sorry, I think my hearing is jacked up," Chase told him over the phone. "What are you talking about? You just proposed to me less than a month ago and now all of a sudden you're seeing another woman? I'm sorry, I'm just not understanding." Chase was dumbfounded.

"No, your hearing is fine. I never should have proposed to you in the first place. That's my fault and my poor decision making and I take complete responsibility for that. But I can't keep secret about what's going on in my life anymore because the woman that I'm seeing has left her spouse as well and we're going to be together."

"Oh, so I see. Both of you are cheaters and you actually think that relationship is going to work? Two cheaters decide to get together? Hilarious," Chase said sarcastically. "Do you honestly think it is going to last. I mean come on?" she mocked him.

"It doesn't matter if it lasts or not. I want to try it out. I'm willing to leave you to do that," Anthony told her.

"Oh, you're so going to regret this. Do you know who I am?"

"I know exactly who you are. That's part of the problem you tell me every day of our lives. So what you made the New York Times bestseller list ten times in a row. So what one of your manuscripts was picked up for a film deal with Paramount. It's as if you have no problem telling me these things every day. But those are just things you've done. I'm more interested in the woman that makes me feel like a king in our house. I feel like there's a power struggle with you and me. Like you want to be the one in the relationship with the pants on all of the time and if that's your position there's no space for me. You can do that by yourself. I'm not needed for that. I need to make that very clear to you and that was ultimately my decision to move on. The woman

I'm dating now has no problem letting me wear the pants in the relationship. She lets me be the man as I should be. The role that I wanted you to let me have that you couldn't seem to let go of. So I bid you farewell as you go figure it out and be the woman and man in a relationship good luck," Anthony told her as he hung up the phone no longer interested in continuing the conversation. He had done what he was supposed to do and that was break off his relationship with Chase so that he could move on to his new relationship.

Chase stared down at the phone in her hand once Anthony hung up. He has some nerve breaking up with me, she thought. Great, just another story for the tabloids. How fantastic. Marcie is going to love this one. Just great. Chase threw the phone at the wall taking sweet pleasure hearing it shatter as all the pieces hit the floor.

The funeral

Chase felt bad. She felt as if she was the only one not shedding a tear in memorandum of her father. Her mother was completely inconsolable; which Chase understood considering their tumultuous history. Sitting behind her black Chanel sunglasses Chase wished she could be anywhere but here. The sooner the minister got on with the eulogy the sooner she would be running down the aisle to get out the church. She didn't realize her father had so many friends. More than 200 people have piled into the church to pay their respects to her sperm donor. She would have just as well not come but she felt like she should be there to support her mom who was taking his death pretty badly. Chase didn't want to be one of the reasons that her mother was worse off. But she was really dealing with her own stuff. Such as Anthony just abruptly rolling out on her talking about he was seeing someone else. The nerve of that guy. I swear right here and missed church she said looking up at the ceiling I will not date another man for as long as I live because they are no good to anyone but themselves. They are selfish and lack any type of respect when it comes to being in a monogamous relationship. And I'm sick of the whole thing. My career will be my new man. At least I trust it. It keeps putting money in my bank account and everything is lovely.

"So what time are we going to the grave site?" Marcie leaned over and whispered into Chase's ear.

"Oh yeah, I don't do those. So we won't be going to the gravesite. I refuse to give this man much more attention than he is deserving of. And that's that. Maybe you and I can hit up an early happy hour or something."

Marcie gazed at Chase as if she were from another planet.

"Happy Hour? You honestly don't want to go to your dad's grave site and pay last respects?" she asked.

"Why would I pay respect to someone I don't respect?" Chase asked her. "I'm perfectly okay. I said all I needed to say the last time we had lunch together and he didn't want to make amends. I'm not interested in anything now that he's gone. I can move on with my life and I can be happy." Chase meant every word. She didn't care that she sounded like a cold-hearted person.

Marcie said, "Well if that's how you feel, it is what it is. I'll make us a reservation somewhere on our way out the door."

"Wonderful then I can tell you all about Anthony and his phone call to me early this morning on top of everything else. He knew today was the day of my dad's funeral and he couldn't resist the urge to put a cherry on top. Happy burial of my dad to me," Chase said in a singsong voice.

"You watch your mouth young lady," Chase's mother Melissa said to her. "I heard everything you said. Mind your manners or you can leave."

Chase sat back in her chair and closed her mouth. She hadn't known that her mother had been listening to her conversation. One thing she had never intended to do was disrespect her mother.

"Yes ma'am. I apologize; I was not trying to be rude at your expense."

"Thank you for that." Melissa told her. Please don't say anything for the rest of the ceremony, thanks," her mother told her.

Chase bowed her head as the minister went on with his sermon and sat in silence as to not offend her mother.

He was there at the funeral. At first something like a mirage. I thought that strange. Why was he here? Either way, now that he was present an introduction must be made. An entryway into the tunnel. He was about to enter into a world of WTF and I couldn't wait.

~ *Chase*

Chapter 2

● ● ●

"**Congratulations on that** piece you did on the survivors of that quake over in Bali."

Flashing a double mint smile in appreciation Theodore shook his boss's hand. "Keep this up and you'll definitely believe in me for CNN soon." Theodore watched as his boss sighed. "Maybe don't keep up the good work. I really don't want to lose you."

"I'll see what I can do," Theodore grinned. Making his way back to his cubicle he was surprised to see a bouquet of yellow long stem roses setting atop his desk.

"So you slinging it like that? You have women buying you flowers now? Who is Chase?"

"You read the card and everything?" Theodore gazed up at his colleague, Matthew. "I mean; can a brother get some privacy around here?"

"Privacy where?" Matthew looked around. "You buggin'. Our cubicles practically kiss each other. There is no privacy to be had in this office."

"I can see that," Theodore responded as he sat in his chair and read the card that Matthew had graciously left on his desk upright.

```
         To the unexpected surprise.
                 ~ Chase
```

Theodore smiled.

"Teeth out and everything," Matthew exclaimed laughing. "She got you drooling."

"I met this girl yesterday at a Happy Hour."

"Oh, that's where you picking up women now," Matthew joked. "Maybe I need to start going to more of those," he laughed.

Teddy chuckled. "I didn't set out to meet anyone. It just happened. She buried her father yesterday."

"Seriously? And she's the one sending you flowers?" Matthew asked incredulously, "What kind of backward courtship is this?"

"Hey, I'm not the one that asked her to send me the flowers," Theodore laughed.

Matthew shook his head, "You playas are all the same."

Teddy stood up out of his chair, "Playa your boy is not. I just be living my life."

"Well obviously I'm living wrong."

"You said it, I didn't," Teddy laughed.

A college graduate from Emory University in Atlanta, Georgia, Theodore loved letting people know that he graduated with a Bachelor of Arts degree with his concentration being English. He wasn't just another black man on the street who had locked up and made it. He'd worked hard for everything that he had and he would let no one deprive him of that.

Dubbed a Shemar Moore look alike by the women during his college days, he tried hard not to let that go to his head. Just because they thought of him as a pretty boy, he didn't have to come off that way. So he worked super hard to overcome that stereotype and let people know that he worked for everything he had. A small-town boy raised by a single mother, he knew what it was like to struggle every day of his life. He knew that he would work extra hard not to have to struggle another day ever again in his life. He thanked God for giving him the talent of writing.

"So what is she like?" Matthew asked.

"Beautiful," Theodore told him. "I can't describe it. But she is beautiful. Inside and out."

"Oh, yeah?"

"Yeah. I mean nothing that I haven't seen before, but I haven't seen it before. If that makes sense."

"Yeah, that makes sense." Matthew told him.

"She may be the new Mrs. Scott you mark my words," Theodore joked.

"Damn. It's like that?" Matt was amazed

"Definitely like that," Teddy laughed.

He loved Matthew like one of his own brothers. He and Matt had been roommates at Emory. Matthew Barone came from a prestigious Italian family that ran Barone Pasta, a restaurant chain throughout the United States and Italy. To say his money was long being an understatement.

****

Dialing the number left on the card from the bouquet of flowers, Theodore waited patiently as the phone rang on the other end.

"Chase Campbell." A sultry voice came across the other end of the line.

"Chase Campbell. As in the Chase Campbell? New York Times bestseller, I have a movie in the works, too? That Chase Campbell?"

Chase smiled on her end of the line. She loved men that did their homework. "The one and only. May I ask who's calling?"

"The one who received an embarrassingly large display of white roses on his desk at work today."

"I still don't compute," She smiled on her side of the phone. Being sarcastic.

"Am I to believe, that you just buy large bouquets of flowers for every man that you meet?" Theodore asked playfully.

"Um, it depends. I've been known to do something of the sort a time or two." Chase laughed out loud this time, "How are you Theodore? I was hoping that you would enjoy the flowers and give me a call."

"It's not every day that a man receives flowers. So you know I had to call and thank you appropriately as well as ask you out to dinner tonight."

"I would definitely love to have dinner with you tonight. Do you have a place in mind?"

"I would like to surprise you if that's okay," Theodore stated.

"That's fine. Do you want to pick me up from the office this evening?"

"Sure let's do that. I look forward to seeing you tonight, Chase."

"I look forward to seeing you as well, Teddy. I like that more than Theodore," Chase laughed.

"Teddy is actually my nickname, so it's okay. See you tonight. I'll pick you up around eight. Text me your address when you have a moment."

"Will do. See you tonight at eight. Bye." Chase hung up the phone smiling. She was excited to go out with Theodore. *Whoa, nothing like a sexy man to get my mouth watering,* she thought.

****

When Theodore arrived to pick up Chase that evening, she was glad that she was always prepared with extra clothing in her office. Tonight she opted for a sexy flirty look. Nothing too dressy, something more casual and hip. She had put on some black jeans with a few cutouts. Not a lot. Just enough to be classy. She had on her Mary Jane Louboutin's and a DVF floral top under a fuchsia blazer. Her hair was swept up on top of her head in a bun and she had a bang that swooped to the side. She flaunted classic diamonds in her ear and a Louis Vuitton clutch in her hands. She was ready to get the evening started.

"You look amazing," Theodore told her as she exited the building and met him at the bottom of the steps.

"You're not too shabby yourself," she told him. And he wasn't. He was dressed very casual as well. Blue jeans, a navy blazer that had a white button down underneath and black KD's on his feet.

"So where you taking me this evening?" she asked as she latched onto the arm he extended out to her.

"Paradise," he told her. He figured with a woman like Chase Campbell on his arm he would have to go the extra mile to charm her. So he waited and kept her firmly in place as the horse and buggy pulled up alongside of them.

"Nice. Very classy, Teddy. Very classy, indeed." She smiled gleefully as he helped her onto the carriage. All her years in New York City and she had never been on a horse and carriage ride. Chase was taking in all of the city lights as the horse and carriage pulled them down the street.

"This is absolutely amazing. Thank you for sharing this experience with me." She smiled into Theodore's eyes.

"Thank you for being the first woman that I've shared it with. Your excitement is making me excited and I'm loving every moment of it." He smiled down at her as he lowered his head to kiss her feeling as if the moment was right.

Chase welcomed his soft lips and closed her eyes. It had been a while since she'd been kissed and felt the warm weight of a man embracing her. She rather enjoyed it. Theodore smelled like a little bit of heaven wrapped up in 6 foot 3 height of a man and she loved every moment of it. This was how a man was supposed to court a woman. She didn't know what Anthony's lame attempts had been.

The horse and carriage came to a stop at Central Park. Theodore unenthusiastically broke his kiss off from Chase. He could kiss her all night and he had to be careful. He wanted to take things slow with her.

"It's time for dinner," he whispered against her lips.

Chase happily opened her cloudy eyes as she gazed longingly into his almond brown ones.

"We're having dinner in the park?" she asked as she took in her surroundings. "How exciting!" Chase squealed. She felt like a schoolgirl.

"Yes, we are," Theodore told her as he led her into the park where he'd had his assistant's lay out a blanket, a basket of food, champagne, strawberries, and an iPad so they could listen to music.

"Oh, how romantic!" Chase exclaimed. She was so excited that she could hardly contain her cheerfulness. "This is amazing."

"I'm glad that you are pleased." Theodore's eyes crinkled in the corners as he smiled warmly at her. He found this woman intoxicating. He could drink in her aura all night.

"I am very pleased. Thank you."

Theodore helped Chase take a seat before sitting down next to her on the blanket. Popping open the bottle of champagne he poured them each a glass and sat the bottle down.

"This is beautiful," Chase told Theodore as she looked up at the sky and smiled at the stars winking at them. She had always been a fan of astronomy.

"The sky is gorgeous. Teddy look," she pointed.

Theodore glanced up at the sky. "Well, so it is. Ms. Campbell. So it is. But not nearly as gorgeous as you are."

He admired the stars with Chase. They spent the rest of the evening enjoying each other's company and making out as if they were high schoolers all over again.

They sit there in glee, while I suffer, the shadowy figure watching them thought from the bushes. *This relationship will have to come to a close. I cannot tolerate these two being together and happy with one another. Their time will come when the inevitable will occur.* The shadowy figure disappeared back amongst the trees as they continued to watch the happy duo.

Chapter 3

· · ·

Chase glanced behind her thinking that she heard footsteps. Lately she had an eerie feeling that she was being followed. Ever since she had gone out with Theodore things were starting to happen. She wasn't trying to be paranoid, but she had a strange feeling lately.

Pulling out her cell phone, she dialed Marcie's number.

"Hey boo, what's going on?" Marcie's cheerful voice came across the line.

"I think I'm being followed," Chase told her bluntly not one to beat around the bush.

"Really? Why? What makes you say that?"

"Just this feeling of unease that I've been having," Chase told her.

"That's crazy. I swear the weirdest things happen to you. Drama on top of drama," Marcie commented.

Chase rolled her eyes. "Can you save me your philosophical BS this morning please? Please? I'm really concerned."

"Seriously?" Marcie finally tuned in to the worry in her friend's voice. "Okay, well why don't I come over and stay with you for little bit. You think that will help?"

"I think that will be a good idea," Chase told her.

"Okay. It's not a problem you know that honey. I love you and if you don't feel safe, we will definitely work it out. Just give me a little bit. I'm out doing some last minute shopping and I'll be right over."

"Great. Sounds like a plan." Chase was grateful that Marcie was her best friend, her road dog. Never letting her go through anything alone.

****

"So, tell me about this Theodore Scott." Marcie laughed as she poured herself another glass of sweet red wine.

Chase actually found herself blushing. "I mean there's nothing to tell...yet. I just find him very interesting."

"Mmmhmmm, I bet you do find him interesting," Marcie grinned. "I'd find him interesting as well, with his sexy ass."

Chase felt her cheeks flaming. She knew that her face had to be lit up like a fireworks display on the Fourth of July from how warm it felt. Cheesing unbelievably hard Chase wanted the conversation to end.

****

Staring at them from outside between the trees through the window, he wondered what they were laughing at. He had never seen her so radiant. Part of him envied that. He wanted to be the one to bring a smile to her face. But he felt as if she had violated him every sense of the word by walking away. That was not their arrangement and she knew better. She knew that there would be consequences to pay for her actions and he would make sure that she felt every single consequence individually if it killed him.

****

"I've been thinking maybe this Theodore thing isn't such a good idea," Chase told Marcie.

Marcie put down her wine glass onto the granite countertop.

"Why do you say that? I'm curious. I can tell that you like him."

"I don't know. Dating has never worked out for me in the past and I don't really see it working now."

"Please tell me that you're not basing your knowledge on that idiot and fool Anthony," Marcie said. "Because clearly he is not someone to compare anyone to unless it's a dog. Anthony needs to get it together, okay? His whole existence bothers me like he smells like trouble I can't believe you dated him as long as you did."

"Kindred spirits, I guess. Believe it or not Anthony had his good moments, you know."

"All I saw from him were a whole bunch of assholes moments. But hey that's me," Marcie said snidely.

"Hey girl, I mean, it is what it is. We're no longer together so it's not a big deal. Anthony can take all his issues to the new woman he's dating and keep it pushing for all I give a damn. He was weak anyway and weak is completely not my style. I think it was just something to do, you know, to get me over my hump of my last ex-boyfriend."

"I have to agree with you on that because you know your choices in men haven't been exactly the best," Marcie pointed out.

"I mean excuse you. But I don't see no man knocking down your door missy." Chase reminded her. "You sure have a strong opinion these days."

"My bad, my bad. I'm just saying. Trying to educate a sister is all."

"Well a sister doesn't need no education, Marcie. I appreciate you, but can you hold the judgment down just a little bit? Please and thank you."

Marcie laughed. "Don't take your little attitude out on me. You know I believe in stating facts. That's all I'm saying."

"Can you please state facts a little more quietly? Please, Marcie please. I beg of you."

"Okay, okay honey. I promise to go easy on you. Though this is just my opinion, I truly believe that you should give Theodore a chance. Let him at least do something bad before you cut him off. Right now, everything seems to be going great, so let it go great. Have a good time. Just enjoy life. It doesn't have to be any pressure. He doesn't have to be your next boyfriend. Just go on a few dates. What's wrong with dating?" Marcie inquired.

"There's nothing wrong with dating," Chase agreed.

"See. So take the pressure off yourself, calm down and just chill out. If you want something to stress out about, it needs to be this new book tour that we're trying to plan and you won't give me the cities you want to go to. Let's focus on that," Marcie quipped.

"Marce, I don't want to talk about work. We enjoying wine down time. There is no work talk during wine down time. There is only us pouring wine and downing it," Chase reminded her.

Marcie laughed. "Girl, you good and crazy. Ok, no work talk tonight. Just male bashing at its finest."

Chase grinned, "I don't want to male bash. I want to love on someone."

Marcie eyed her suspiciously. "I hope you don't think you're going to be cuddling up next to me for some love cause ain't nobody got time for that, boo boo. I'm strictly on my dick game."

Chase burst out laughing, sitting her wine down in the process. "Why are you stupid? Goodness! I do not need your cuddling services, thank you very much. I will do just fine."

"Oh, okay. I was just making sure. I'd hate to have to fight my bestie up in here. I mean, could you imagine what I would have to tell the cops? I'd be like my bestie tried to hump me officer and I had to let her know I'm strictly dickly, so I smacked her across her forehead with a dildo," Marcie laughed.

"I can't stand you," Chase responded holding her stomach from laughing so hard. "Girl, you are something else. I needed this tonight because I have been on edge lately."

"I knew I could sense that. Now grab that bottle and let's go get our 'Netflix & hill' on."

"I hate that term so much," Chase told her.

"That's okay, you can hate it. But you love me, so it's all good," Marcie informed her.

"Touché, my favorite Puerto Rican. Touché'."

Chapter 4

• • •

"Baby I made a huge mistake. I want to get back together." Nikki's voice oozed with sexiness.

"Nikki, I don't have time for your games today," Theodore told her. "Where the boys? It's my day to take them out."

"They're at my mom's house. I wanted to talk to you today."

"I'm not in the mood to talk to you. Why you playing games?"

"I'm not playing games, baby. I'm serious. I want to get back together. I'm being as honest with you as I can."

Theodore shook his head not even remotely interested in what she had to say.

"Aren't you the same woman who stormed into this room not too long ago to tell me that our relationship was over? Now you're back in my face saying what exactly? I'm not exactly sure what I'm supposed to do with that information," Teddy told her.

"I made a huge mistake. Colossal. It's so huge that I will do whatever you want me to do so that we can be together. Here, you need a foot massage? You want me to rub your feet scrub your back, cut your hair? Baby, whatever you need. I love you and want us to be together."

Theodore paused to make it seem like he was thinking about it. "You know what that's okay. I'm good. I don't need to be with someone who has no problem walking away from a relationship with me without even trying to work it out. I asked you to go to counseling with me. I was willing to forgive you and your little indiscretion and say whatever to hell with it. We got a family, let's work this thing out, and what did you do? You told me to get out of the house. You practically tried to kick me out of the family. There's nothing you can do for me at this point. Nothing at all. The only thing the two of us can do together is co-parent even though that's going to take some working itself out because obviously you don't know how to do it since the boys aren't here today."

Nikki allowed herself to burst into tears hoping that would help to persuade him.

"Nikki, please kill the drama. I'm not interested. At this moment, I'm seeing somebody so there's really nothing else for us to talk about. This is somebody that I've been wanting to see. She appreciates me and it's nice to feel appreciated. She's not the type of woman to say all I wanted to divorce because I've been seeing someone new and what we have is over. She's not that type of person at all. That's a character flaw and I wish I had seen that in you a long time ago. That's my fault then, but getting back with you would be my fault now and I just can't have that happen. I'm sorry. I truly am. I hate to leave you like this, but I've got to do what's best for me and my family and right now that's just making sure that I can be the best me that I can possibly be. Without you. So you can put your waterworks away. They don't move me one-way or the other. They're not going to weigh in your favor and I do believe in your famous words, 'I'm done here.' I'll stop by your moms and pick up the boys."

"Absolutely not. You're going to listen to what I have to say."

"Nikki, no. We're separated and headed for divorce. I'm actually excited about it now and there's nothing left to say. You can't hold me hostage here. I'm gone. Take care of yourself, okay? I really want you to do that. I love you no matter what. I'll always love you. Don't ever forget that."

Teddy told her before giving her a kiss on the cheek and leaving the house.

No sooner had Theodore returned home without his sons, because Nikki's mother hadn't been home, did his doorbell ring.

Teddy sighed in annoyance when he saw who was on the other side.

"What is it, Nikki?" Teddy asked her as he opened the door only a crack so that she wouldn't be able to force her way in.

"I'm confused, Teddy. Where is my money?" Nikki's voiced oozed with sarcasm. "You be running around these streets like you a big baller. Journalist of the year and what not. Hanging at all these celebrity parties." Nikki held out her hand. "So, where's my money?"

"I don't know what money you speak of," Theodore told her not in the least impressed with her theatrics.

"Yeah. Okay, okay." Nikki shook her head jumping up and down. "You keep playing with me and you'll see what's going to happen."

Closing his eyes and rubbing his forehead Theodore prayed for someone to shoot him right at that moment. He wasn't feeling up to the task of handling Nikki. He had a date to get ready for.

"Is this what you dropped by for?" He was indifferent to her at this point. "The courts decided what you would get paid as you wished for them to do, so why you over here bothering me?" he asked her.

"I see you trying to be real cute all of a sudden. Let me tell you don't play with me, alright?"

Teddy sighed, exacerbated. Today just wasn't his day. "Nikki, why are you here? We've been to court. Your check is coming for my son's. You know I'm happy to take care of them. So, what is it that you really want?"

"I want you to come home."

"I am home," he reminded her.

"Not here," she said trying to glance through the doorway since her hadn't invited her inside. "I mean our home."

"We don't have a home and I don't have time for this. I have something to do."

"Oh yeah, like what?" Nikki had her hand on her hip. "Hang with that little Miss Erika Badu chick I seen you with?"

Theodore smirked, finally they had hit gold.

"So that's why you're here. You've been spying in me."

"I sure the hell have and I can't believe you. You're not divorced yet! You should not be dating."

"If I'm not mistaken, you chose to divorce me. Not vice versa. Now you standing at my door looking foolish and pathetic and I freaky don't have time for your dreams today. I've got to go." Teddy was bored with the whole conversation. He closed the door in her face with a snap. Nikki was going to be a problem, but he would have to focus on her later. Chase was waiting.

"I've missed you," Teddy whispered into Chase's ear when he picked her up for their dinner date.

"I missed you as well." Chase was appalled that she actually had the audacity to blush. But she wasn't lying. She honestly didn't miss him. It was nice to be honest about it.

So where do you have at a time off to today? Firmly believe that there is no way you can top our first date. She laughed.

"You'd be surprised. Don't underestimate me," Teddy told her with a grin.

Chase chose to remain quiet wondering what he could possibly have up his sleeve. But she was anxious to find out. So far into their dating, so good.

Theodore had a real treat for Chase tonight. He couldn't wait to share the evening with her.

"Are we heading towards Broadway?" Chase asked him excitedly. She loved Broadway.

Theodore winked at her but remained silent.

When their car pulled up in front of the Gershwin Theatre Chase had to keep her composure to not swoon in the car.

"Please, tell me you didn't," she said in excitement. "How did you know this was my favorite play of all time?" Chase grinned widely at him.

"A little birdie may have whispered a little something to me," Theodore admitted. "Or I just may be that good." He smiled.

Chase playfully hit him on his chest. She said unable to contain herself any longer "Let's go, let's go. We're in Wicked land."

"Wicked land, huh?"

"Absolutely. You gonna' learn you something today in case you don't know so. This is so fabulous! You're the best boyfriend ever."

Chase paused when she let the words flip out of her mouth. *Now where did that come from,* she thought. *Am I even ready for a boyfriend? It's only our second date. Oh my gosh. What is he thinking? He probably thinks I'm an idiot.*

Theodore smiled down at Chase. "That seems like a nice title to have." He grabbed her hand. "Now, let's go inside before we miss the beginning."

Chase smiled in relief. "Kay," she told him.

Chapter 5

● ● ●

"Thank you for coming out shopping with me today. I really need some new clothes."

"New clothes to go with your new man," Marcie laughed.

"Something like that," Chase laughed "You funny."

"Anytime with you is a great time. Plus, I love Neiman Marcus. My favorite store of all time."

"You just like spending my hard earned money," Chase told her.

"Um, excuse you." Marcie eyed her with a grin. "It's the hard earned money that my hard earned job

& connections got you. Don't be trying to play me. I work hard for my twenty percent."

Chase nodded in agreement, "You're right. You do, but you still like spending my money." She winked at her.

"Well...true. Anytime I don't have to spend my money is a good time," Marcie laughed.

"I bet it is." Chase rolled her eyes. "Let's head to Louis Vuitton. There's this bag I've been eyeing."

"Can we eat first? You've had me out all day. I'm starving!" Marcie reminded her about food because if she didn't Chase was likely to not have them eat till the evening sometime and she couldn't have that. She was a cranky hungry person.

"Alright, alright. Where would you like to go to get your grub on?"

"Let's go to The Cheesecake Factory. I've been waiting to get back there."

"Really, Marce? You go there at least once a week. I'm sure it hasn't changed that drastically since your last excursion."

"Hush, you don't know me like that." Marcie smiled at her. "Let's go."

"After you, my dear." Chase waved her past.

****

"Thank you for taking the time to meet with me today," Nikki told Teddy. She had invited him out to lunch and he had happily agreed to which she was thankful.

"It's the least I can do," he told her. He had only done so as a means to keep the peace so that he could continue to see his sons with no drama. "So what's going on with you?" he asked her. "Why did you request this meeting?"

"Because I've been thinking lately," Nikki began, "I want you take me seriously since I don't believe that you did before." She studied his face before continuing, "I don't really want to break up anymore."

Theodore looked at her as if she has lost her mind. She's the one that requested the divorce after telling him that she had a boyfriend and wanted out. And now at this stage he was not interested in anything she had to say that involved them remaining in a relationship together. He'd been devastated when he found out about her affair. But now that he was out of the situation and far removed with a new girlfriend, there was nothing she could do to win him back. He was ready to move on with his life.

"What do you have to say about that?" she asked.

"Nothing that I haven't said honestly," Teddy told her. "There's nothing left to say at this point. I'm not in agreement with you and I'm enjoying being single again."

Nikki set back in her chair and just looked at him. "So is this how you want to play it?" she asked him not in the least bit impressed with his mood.

"I'm not playing at anything." Teddy told her. "I want you to be happy, I want to be happy, and we don't make each other happy together. So let's just keep it moving. I like the arrangement that we have now," he said.

"So it doesn't matter what I think or feel? That's just it, huh?" Nikki was honestly surprised. She was sure he would hold out for a moment but she had no idea that he would dig his heals in and prefer to be single than to be with her.

Nikki couldn't sit there and make it seem as if she wasn't in her feelings. She definitely was. She'd been stupid to let her man go and now she could tell he wanted to be gone for good. But she was going to do everything in her power to stop that from happening.

****

As the hostess began walking them to their table, Chase passed by a familiar face.

"Teddy. Is that you?" She stopped when she saw him turn around to face her.

She knew her face displayed one of shock. He was sitting at the table with another woman.

Teddy jumped up out of his seat once he saw Chase approach the table.

"Chase. It's good to see you," he said, feeling guilty as if he were caught doing something wrong.

"Hi." She eyed him inquisitively.

"This is Nikki, my soon to be ex-wife and mother to our two boys. Nikki, this is my girlfriend, Chase." His eyes pleaded with Nikki's in an attempt to make her behave herself.

"Ohhhh. So this is the little girlfriend I keep hearing all about. Mmmm."

"Hold up. What do you mean mmm?" Marcie jumped in. She was not going to let this Pop Tart of a chick disrespect her girl Chase.

Chase quickly stepped in-between Marcie and the woman Theodore had introduced as Nikki.

"Did I understand you correctly?" Chase addressed Teddy. "Did you say that this woman is your wife? As in, you are married and not single?"

"Yes, I am his wife. Don't talk about me like I'm not here."

"We're getting a divorce." Theodore said as he ignored Nikki's outburst.

"Why didn't you mention this to me before?" a wounded Chase asked Theodore. "Honesty is everything to me."

Teddy could see that Chase's feelings were hurt but he knew couldn't explain himself entirely at the moment because Nikki was hell bent on causing a scene and he wanted to avoid that at all costs.

"Please allow me to explain everything to you later. We're only meeting right now to discuss the boys. It's not a romantic dinner or anything." he added in for emphasis.

Chase just shook her head. "I told you I don't trust men," she said to Marcie. "They never tell the damn truth. No matter how nice they seem at first. It all seems like one big joke and us woman arc just a pawn in their little game."

Chapter 6

● ● ●

"It's not what you think it is, period." Teddy told her as he ran behind her as she stormed out of the restaurant.

As Chase stormed passed Teddy out of the restaurant, she couldn't begin to understand why she was so upset. She had just met Teddy. It's not as if he owed her an explanation. He was allowed to date whomever he wanted to date. It just hurt her nerves how comfortable he seemed with the woman that he was having a lunch with. That's what Chase was pissed off about and had led to her leaving the restaurant.

"Chase, will you listen to me?" Theodore couldn't understand why she was in such an uproar. She wouldn't even let him explain his case. "It's not what you think it is. Listen to what I'm telling you."

"I don't want to hear it," she told him.

"Can you please hear me out? That's all I ask." He finally caught up to her and grabbed her arm forcing her to stop, bringing her around to stand in front of him so that they could be face to face. He willed her to listen.

Chase maintained a look of indifference on her face. As far as she was concerned, all men were just the same and got on her nerves.

"That woman in there is soon to be my ex-wife."

"I can't believe that you're married?" she whispered.

"Separated," Theodore clarified. "We are getting divorced. We've already worked out everything. All that we're waiting on is the paperwork."

. Chase was speechless. Not once had he mentioned to her that he had been married, was married, and in the midst of a divorce.

"We were actually meeting just to go over custody of the kids. She wants more money but the judge had already decided what her payments are going to be."

"Kids?" Chase questioned. "You never mentioned kids."

"I only didn't mention them because we had just started dating. I didn't see the point just yet since I was just getting to know you. There's no reason to bombard you with all my problems right out front especially if you plan on being around. That means there will be plenty of time for us to have a discussion about all that stuff.

"You doing okay over here?" Marcie approached slowly figuring she had given Theodore ample time to explain himself.

"Yeah, I'm good," Chase told her. "Just ready to go. I have no time for someone else's dreams today."

"I hear you on that, sista'. Let's dodge this place. Maybe this will cure my Cheesecake Factory infatuation," Marcie said as she looped her arm through Chase's and gave Teddy the evil eye.

Teddy bowed out gracefully. He knew he was not going to be able to make any head way with Chase tonight. He was going to give her some breathing room as he tended to Nikki.

"Yo, what was your deal tonight? You think that the way you behave was funny?" Theodore was upset and he knew shouting at Nikki wouldn't solve his problems but he needed her to understand that he was pissed off.

MY BOYFRIEND'S WIFE 2

"What you yelling at me for? All I did was state facts if you learn how to tell the truth may be a little girlfriend wouldn't be in her feelings now with she? All she would have done was rolled up on the situation that she already knew about and then you wouldn't be in the doghouse as you are right now. Not that I care either way," Nikki told him.

"If this is your way of trying to get back with me, you are sadly mistaken. You will never get me at this rate."

"Why, Teddy dear, would I help you save face with your current girlfriend while you're having dinner with your wife? That doesn't make sense in any language. I don't care if I spoke Spanish, French, Italian, or whatever. It doesn't make sense. Even you know me better than that," she told him, smirking as she said it.

"Hey yo, Nik, it's not funny." He could see that she was thoroughly enjoying his discomfort.

"You really mad are you?" Nikki asked him. "Well, I really don't know what to tell you honey. It's your own fault so you cannot blame this on me. I'm not the way. I didn't contact her. I didn't go to her house, or her job, and knock on her door. I didn't do any of that. I was just at a restaurant with my baby daddy slash husband talking about our life and what we're going to do from here on out. Not my fault you don't know how to be honest." She smiled up at him.

"No, I can't do this with you today. I'm 'bout to roll."

"Suit yourself. But you are more than welcome to stay," Nikki told him as she began unbuttoning her shirt.

"Don't even bother removing your clothes." Theodore told her in disgust. "I'm not interested in anything you offering. I'll be by to get the boys this weekend. Have them here and not off at your mother's please. Lata," Teddy bid her farewell as he exited the house.

Chapter 7

● ● ●

Walking the busy streets in New York, Chase was surprised to see Nikki waiting outside of Marcie's building when she came down. Currently on cloud nine from her agency allowing her a little bit of downtime while she tried to figure out what she wanted to do after the storm was over, she was elated, and she really didn't want anyone to mess up her high.

Shoot, what does this girl want today? I really don't want her to ruin this for me, Chase thought.

Attempting to brush past Nikki as if she didn't see her, Chase tried to keep going but Teddy's soon to be ex-wife was having none of it.

"Yo. I know you see me standing here," Nikki yelled at Chase as she grabbed her by the arm.

Chase was many things but a punk she was not and she wasn't going to have Nikki out here putting her hands on her in the middle of the street.

"You have lost your mind just tell her if she pushed Nikki back to get away from her. Don't you ever put your hands on me. It's not often I get messy but I will eff you up in these streets."

"I mean, if you want to get thrown in jail for hitting a pregnant woman by all means attempt to eff me up in these streets but sweetie don't get your feelings hurt. I may be small in appearance, but my hands get it done quite nicely."

"I feel sorry for whoever got you pregnant. I'll pray for him."

"Well, you'll be praying for Teddy." Nikki capped back with a smile.

"What the hell are you talking about, crazy lady? Teddy would never put his hands on you even to scratch you. How could he possibly get you pregnant?" Chase wasn't in the mood for shenanigans today. Especially with over-the-top dramatic baby mamas who didn't know they place. "And funny, be poppin up on me in the street. I can tell you not really about that life." Chase warned her.

"You may want to get your facts checked, honey." Nikki smiled a Colgate grin at her. "This is definitely Teddy's baby. I have no reason to lie. He is my husband after all. You're the one that's over here been a side hoe," Nikki accused Chase.

"Side hoe? You must have me completely effed up. I have never been anyone's side so as you call it. You're the one who's trying to hold on to a man that you say you wanted to divorce. That's your bad.

You cheated on him, he didn't cheat on you honey and now you're grasping at straws trying to get him to stay while you pick the right one this time. Cuz I don't have time for these crazy games. I'm a grown ass woman. If you want to play these high school games, you're going to have to play on by yourself. Whatever you and Teddy got going is you and Teddy business but at the end of the day. I'm not his side hoe, I'm not his wannabe, I'm not his baby mama, I'm his girlfriend. We holding it down and that's just what it is. So miss me with all your bull. I ain't here for none of that. Handle your business elsewhere. Your problem not with me your problem is with your children's father so y'all deal with that and leave me out of it. Have a good day."

"Yo, mami. You good?" Marcie asked walking up the sidewalk.

"No, I'm good. This chick just over here clowning that's all. Nothing to worry about. I've already handled it."

"You ain't handle a damn thing," Nikki screamed. "Don't be thinking you just going to dismiss me like that and that's how it's going to go down. You can try to ignore me and say what you want to say but the baby is coming now deal with that," Nikki told her as she hocked spit on Chase.

Before Marcie could stop her, Chase jumped into Nikki and began swinging on her until Nikki fell to the pavement.

"Dumb bitch. I don't care if you are pregnant. Never in your life will you spit on another human being. Oh, I taught that as something today," Chase yelled as Nikki curled up in a ball attempting to shield her stomach.

"Come on, Cha Cha. Leave her be. I think she learned her lesson," Marcie said as she pulled Chase up off of Nikki.

"This girl had me completely fucked up," Chase screamed.

"She doesn't anymore. Trust me. Come on. We got to get out of here." Marcie wanted to get Chase as far away from Nikki as possible before the feds came and locked everyone up.

Chapter 8

● ● ●

"**I am floored with this** turn of events. How is it then Nikki is popping up on me in the middle the street talking about she's pregnant with your baby? You have some explaining to do. I don't do drama. I told you this in the beginning and yet here we are caught in the middle of your drama. I'm not impressed."

Chase folded her arms as she stared Theodore down as he stood in her kitchen looking like a hurt puppy. She had no remorse for him. He needed to start explaining himself before she put him out of the house.

"You have five minutes explaining then I'm done with this," she told him, thinking to herself, *this is exactly why I said I didn't want to date anyone else. Men are messy.*

Theodore sheepishly looked at the floor.

"I know all of this seems crazy but you know Nikki. She just says stuff out her mouth sometimes not really thinking about the consequences."

"Okay, I really don't need a blow by blow of Nikki. What I need to know is if it's true or not because that determines how I deal with you. I could care less about you guy's relationship."

"From what she tells me it's true. But hold on," Theodore said as Chase unfolded her arms and looked as if she was about to put him out." I had some sperm saved at a sperm bank and she took it upon herself to have herself impregnated."

Taking a deep breath Chase forced herself to remain calm.

"I can't do this anymore, Teddy. It's just too much. You have way too much going on in your personal life and I really think you need to focus on that and whatever it is you choose to do is up to you but I don't think I should be held up in the middle of it. I just don't believe that it will be fair to me. It will however Nikki got pregnant she still pregnant and you're going to the type of person you are you're going to want to be around to raise your kid just like you're around for the other two and I just don't see myself going into a serious relationship with someone who has a brand new baby on the way that doesn't even sound right leaving my lips out and been out loud and the universe to hear. I definitely wish you guys the best. I want you to work it out or whatever it is you're going to do. I just...I can't be a part of this. I just can't. Chase wanted to make it clear that she was just done with everything.

"How can you say that?" Theodore asked her. "I'm trying to explain to you what was going on and how everything went down and I really need you to understand right now. I need you to be on my side and see what I'm telling you to be true."

"I don't believe what you told me it isn't true. I just know myself. It's just too much, it's too much. I have your wife slash ex-wife slash separated slash baby mama popping up on me in the streets. Are you crazy? It's too much, it's too much. I don't have the time to be having this type of drama in the newspaper. I can lose some of my contract with this type of behavior, I cannot be fighting someone in the street and today I feel like I was going to come that she didn't tell me she was pregnant and I just choose not to be about that life anymore I'm a grown woman and grown woman she was the walk away from issues day for see happening."

Theodore reach for Chase but she backed up just out of his reach.

"I would like for you to go now. I just...there's nothing we can do it here."

"I can't do that," Theodore told her, "because if I leave right now, I know that it's really over and you're not going to allow me to come back and I can't have that."

She stared up at him. "What is it that you want for my life? I have nothing to give to you. I don't want to do this. Do you really want to stand there and force someone to be with you than sitting here telling you that they don't want to be in this situation at all?"

"Yes. I know that is selfish," Theodore stated, "but I would really like for you to give me the opportunity to prove to you that is not what you think it is and that this is just a small stepping stone. I'll be divorced soon and will baby get passes and who knows maybe one day we'll laugh about this."

"I seriously doubt that," Chase told him. "I mean I may not know the law that great, but I do know that

MYCHEA

a pregnant wife does not get a divorce. The judge won't grant that unless you can prove that you didn't sleep with her and how do you prove that?"

"I hadn't thought of that." Teddy told her honestly. "All I know is I will do my best to make this divorce happen quickly so that you and I can proceed to live our lives in peace."

"There is no life to live," Chase told him. "I don't want to be a part of any of this. I want you to fix it first and then we'll go from there but I really don't want to be attached to this. Can you understand that?"

"I'm not giving up. You're my woman and we're going to stay that way."

Chase sighed in exasperation. She could see that clearly Teddy refused to take no for an answer. He just wasn't having it. And she would be lying if she didn't say his persistence wasn't a turn on. She was so used to guys leaving as quickly as they could. At least Teddy with role in the fight with for something he believed in where there was a losing battle or not. She had to give him an 'A' for effort. He was trying.

"Ok, you. I will give you a little time to work this thing out but not a lot. And if I see that you can't get a grasp on it I'm going to have to let you go. I have to move on with my life. I refuse to be enslaved to your problems and that's just what it is."

"That's fine, I can handle that. Thank you for the opportunity to prove myself."

****

Chase answered the door when she heard a knock on it.

Checking through the peephole, she sighed in exasperation wondering if she had the energy to deal today.

"Anthony, what do you want?" she asked as she opened the door and stood in the frame refusing to let him in.

"I want an opportunity to talk to you," he replied sheepishly.

"I'm not interested," Chase told him as she attempted to close the door.

"Come on Cha. Just hear me out for a second."

"Why do you think that you deserve for me to hear what you have to say?" She looked at him passively. wishing he would remove himself from her doorstep. "I'm still reeling from our last conversation where you just rolled out on me without a true explanation. Just…we're done. See ya."

"What happened to your new little boo thing? Because I figure this has everything to do with the two of you are probably not together anymore. Which is such a tragic shame actually because what will you do now?"

"Come on, Cha." Anthony hung his head down. "Don't do me like this."

"Don't do you like what?" Now he was beginning to get on Chase's nerves. The audacity of him to imply that she was in some way hurting him when he was the one that walked out of her life. not vice versa. "Leave you hanging like you did me?" Chase crossed her arms over her chest.

"That's not what I meant," Anything began.

"Then what exactly did you mean? Inquiring minds would like to know. Please break it all the way down for me. Because I'm obviously having a hard time understanding."

Anthony looked at her, "You're being very difficult for no reason."

"Oh, I have plenty of reason," Chase cut him off. "You men think y'all can do whatever you want to do and we'll just be here ready to pick up the pieces regardless of your actions."

"That's not what we think. I promise you. Our thought process never makes it that far."

Anthony wiped his hands over his face realizing this was going to be a lot harder than he originally thought.

"Tony, what is it?" Chase softened her tone a little. She could tell he was struggling. And she wasn't completely heartless. She had loved him not too long ago.

"The chick went off and got pregnant by her baby daddy or husband. Whatever you want to call him."

"Let me guess. She just up and left you hanging, huh? Doesn't feel so nice, does it?" Chase was unsympathetic. She had her own issues to deal with. "And then in your current state, you thought that you could just come running back to me and his ole Cha would just take you back in with open arms. Is that it?"

Anthony looked hopeful.

"Well, you are sadly mistaken, boo. Love don't live here anymore." And she slammed the door shut, happy to move on with her afternoon.

The nerve of him, she thought, before turning her attention to cleaning her place. She had neglected it for much too long.

Chapter 9

• • •

"Don't scream," a voice came from behind her.

Marcie whipped around with a knife in her hand that she had been chopping the lettuce with and began stabbing the person in the chest. No one was supposed to be in her house. She did not play that.

"MARCIE, WHAT THE FUCK! STOP! IT'S ME TONY. PLEASE STOP!"

Marcie's arm stopped mid stroke as she heard Anthony's voice.

"Oh my gosh, what are you doing here Tony? What the hell? We gotta call 911! I got to get you to the hospital. Oh my gosh."

"I feel so bad. This is crazy." She grabbed her cell phone dialing the operator as she watched the pool of blood oozing from his body.

"The ambulance is coming. Shit. Why would you be in my house unannounced? " Marcie kneeled down on the floor next to Anthony.

"Anthony keep talking to me," she told him as he gasped for oxygen. "Please talk to me."

Anthony tried, but he was getting weaker by the moment. He could literally hear the beating of his heart pounding in his eardrums. *I'm dying*, he thought, as he passed out.

****

"What in the world happened?" Chase asked Marcie when she visited her at the jailhouse.

"I don't know." Marcie exclaimed. "One moment I was cutting lettuce and then the next I heard this whispering voice talking about some 'Don't scream' and I turned around and started stabbing his ass 'cuz you know I don't play that.

Wanna' know why I supposed to be in my house but me he shoulda' came over unannounced like. I'm sorry that it was Anthony but you can't be popping up in people houses like that. It's breaking and entering." Marcie looked at Chase matter-of-factly.

"Yeah, I understand that, but now you're in jail," Chase pointed out.

"That's because they think we had an argument and I stabbed him in the heat of the moment. I keep trying to tell these geniuses that he broke into my damn place."

"Let me see if I can bail you out of here. This is craziness."

"I'm sorry, Chase. I know this must be tearing you apart. I really didn't know that it was him."

"I know you didn't. I'm a see about bailing you out, and then I'm going to make my way to the hospital to check on his status."

"I just accused Theodore of having too much drama and now look at this crazy situation we got going on. Unbelievable," Chase sighed in resignation. She needed a vacation. Everything was beginning to overwhelm her.

Chase sat at the front of the bonds place waiting for Marcie to come around. She had made her bail and now they needed to be on their way to the hospital to check on Anthony to make sure he was going to live through his battle with Marcie.

"I swear, God, please don't let anything else happen today. I'm not sure that I can take it."

"Get girl, thanks for bailing me out. You ready?"

"Yes, let's go. I never want to come here again."

As soon as they reached the doors of the building, Chase saw cameras going off and reporters everywhere.

"Chase, is it true your boyfriend is in the hospital in critical condition due to your best friend stabbing him?"

"Chase, why didn't you go straight to the hospital to make sure he was okay? It was more important to bail out your friend that stabbed him rather than make sure that he was going to live or die?"

Chase cut her eyes at Marcie as they tried to outrun the reporters. In her haste to get to Marcie she hadn't thought to rent a car for the evening. As a misfortune of forgetting that step, reporters were literally chasing her down the street. *I can't believe that this is happening*, she thought. My own agent or me in this situation. This is bullshit.

Chase was beyond pissed off. She needed peace in her life and this was not the way to go about it. She was worried about Anthony. She was worried about her future with Teddy. Didn't know what was going on. She was trying to figure out if she was mad at Marcie our not for putting her in this situation. There were just a lot of thoughts running through her mind that she had to fix it down and figure out a way to the fact that all she felt like she doesn't have a moment to breathe today. *This should does not be happening to anyone*, she thought to herself.

I cannot continue to live this way. I just can't. There has got to be a silver lining somewhere. There's a rainbow, there's a sun? Somewhere on this earth and I won't stop until I find it. I have got to get away from these crazy people in my life. They're going to drive me absolutely wild.

****

"So just because I no longer want to be with you, you go get yourself stabbed and almost killed. I swear." Chase smiled. "The extremes you men will go through to get some attention is ridiculous."

Sitting down in the chair next to his bed as the heart monitor beeped at a steady pace, Chase wondered if Anthony could hear her.

Marcie had done him a good amount of damage. He was lucky she had missed an artery. But serves him right for breaking into people's homes unannounced. *Who does that,* she thought. Only the clinically insane. Shoot. Marcie owns a gun. He was lucky she hadn't blown his entire head off in the grand scheme of things.

Reaching for his hand, she held it in hers hoping that he would give some acknowledgement of feeling her presence.

"It helps if you talk to him."

Chase jumped at the sound of the nurse's voice. "You think so?" she asked as the nurse checked Anthony's vitals.

"I know so darling. Go ahead and give it a try. It'll make you and him feel a whole lot better," she advised Chase as she exited the room.

Seeing Anthony hooked up to all of the tubes made him seem so helpless to Chase. She felt bad that he was in this predicament. Even though he'd brought it upon himself by underestimating Marcie's level of crazy, Chase still didn't want him stuck in the hospital like this.

Chase leaned in so close that her lips gazed Anthony's ear.

"Oh Tony, look what you've gone and got yourself into. I never wanted anything bad to happen to you. And yet here we are." Chase gently ran her hands down the side of his face. "You know you have to survive this, right? Life just won't be the same if you're not here to harass me every step of the way. I can't imagine a world without you in it. So you get better and I mean get better sooner than later. Don't drag it out just because you like me coming up here so you can listen to the sound of my voice."

At that moment chance felt a very light pressure as Anthony attempted to squeeze her hand.

Chase smiled. "Well look at that. The nurse was right. Seems like you can hear me after all." She allowed her lips to graze his cheek. "I have to go, but you get better soon okay. Fight through this. I love you." She pecked his cheek one more time before leaving the hospital for the evening.

Chapter 10

● ● ●

Teddy walked into his old brownstone that he used to share with Nikki amazed by how quiet it was. That wasn't normal because usually the boys were running around acting crazy while Nikki was yelling at them. There was always some noise going on. The quiet is why Theodore began to worry. The quiet is why everything seemed out of place and out of the ordinary. There was no such thing as quiet and household what boys in and making loud. He knew without a shadow of the doubt that something was very wrong. Walking slowly through the eerily still house a feeling of dread overcame him. Take her and put his finger on it but he just knew but everything in his body was telling him that life was about to change and would never be the same again.

Continuing through the house, he noticed how clean it was. Clean wasn't exactly Nikki's forte. That had been one of the issues in their relationship that he always had with her.

"Nikki!" he shouted out through the house as he continued walking in the direction of their old bedroom. Stopping to glance into each of the boy's room he noticed they were nowhere to be found either which was weird because he was here to pick them up for his weekend with them.

Opening Nikki's bedroom because the door was slightly ajar Teddy's face hit the floor. Lying on the bed in a pool of blood was his family. Every single one of them. The boys and Nikki. Regretting eating breakfast that morning Teddy turned his head to the side as he regurgitated his meal.

HE then ran over to the bed to see if he could detect movement from any of them or to see if they were breathing. He had to force himself to hold the bile in his throat under control, which was proving to be a hard feat to accomplish.

Pulling out his cell phone, he dialed 9-1-1.

"Please come quickly. My family has been murdered," Theodore managed to push the words out of his mouth unable to believe that he had said the words at all.

The scene was gruesome and beyond anything he had ever seen before in his life.

Climbing onto the bed, he wished he could die right there with his family as well. Whoever had done this was a monster. There was no doubt in Teddy's mind.

Nikki's abdomen was sliced open and crisscrossed like a T. He couldn't believe that someone would hate her so much to do something like this.

There was no baby now, you could guarantee that. And then he took in his boy's appearances. Both of them appeared to be sleeping peacefully at first but they were laying on their sides and you could see the blood pooling from an open wound on their throat.

Teddy lay in the blood with his family unable to let them go. Still having a hard time believing.

"Sir, you're going to have to go with the police."

So consumed was he with his agony he hadn't even heard the sirens or the police and EMTs arrive.

"I can't leave them," he sobbed. "I can't leave my family. Can someone just kill me too.? I don't want to be here anymore. Just kill me. Kill me now." He refused to move away from his family.

"Sir," a female officer came to him, "you really have to move out the way so that the EMTs can try to do whatever they can for your family, okay? Come with me," she said softly and patiently, reaching down to grab his arms and guide him to his feet.

Teddy stood up slowly. It was killing him inside.

"The officers outside are going to ask you a couple questions, okay? Do you think you're up to it?"

Teddy didn't know what he was up for. He just wanted to stop crying. He willed himself to focus.

He nodded his head. "Yes," he gasped. "I can answer a few questions."

"Good. Follow me outside," the nice officer told him.

"This here is Officer Bryant. He's going to ask you a few questions just to get your take on what happened, okay?" She patted him on the back and guided him to the edge of the sidewalk.

Teddy nodded again knowing he had to be a sad sight to see. He could feel the puffiness around his eyes from crying. He needed to get away from this place.

"I'm Officer Bryant. How you holding up?"

Teddy took in the tall, older white officer with the friendly blue eyes. Something about the manmade Teddy feel comfortable speaking with him.

"Not too good," Teddy told him honestly in a wavery voice. "That's my family in there." He felt a fresh bout of tears descend his face.

"I know this is difficult for you," Officer Bryant told him as he patted his back in comfort. "You think you can handle giving me a run through of what happened and how you came to find this scene?"

Teddy closed his eyes and nodded again. "I can do this," he spoke softly.

"I came by today because it's my day to get my sons. The plan was for me to pick them up and take them back to my place to spend the weekend. When

I first stepped foot on the premises I knew something was wrong. The house appeared to be too quiet. In a home with boys or kids in general, there is never silence to be had unless the kids are sleep. It was just very calm," he told Officer Bryant who was writing everything down on his pad.

"So I called out Nikki's name and didn't receive a response, which is not normal either because Nikki is hell bent on us saving our marriage so she was over eager to please me anyway."

"Am I to understand that you two were in the process of reconciliation?" Officer Bryant inquired glancing up from his writing pad.

Teddy shook his head. "No, nothing like that. I have a girlfriend. But Nikki doesn't care," he shrugged. "She wants what she wants when she wants it. But then, don't we all."

"Tell me more about your girlfriend. What's her name?" Officer Bryant interrupted.

"Her name is Chase. Chase Campbell. She's a writer and producer."

"Yeah." Officer Bryant nodded. "I've heard about her. She's a special case that one."

"What do you mean by that?" Teddy eyed Officer Bryant.

"She's had a few run-ins with the law through the years. Back to your story. So, you called out to Nikki and then what happened?"

"When I didn't receive a response I began walking through the house looking for everyone. I checked the boys' room and then I noticed Nikki's door was open slightly, so I pushed it open and entered and there lay my family. Just add you find them upstairs. I lay down with them in disbelief." Teddy told him explaining away his bloody clothes. "Then I dialed 911and here you are."

"I'm sorry about your loss, sir. We're going to have you come down to the station and do an official statement. You think you're up for that?"

"Yes. I can handle that. Let's go on down," Teddy told him as he cooperated fully with the beginning of the investigation.

****

Funeral

"Man, I never thought the next time I saw you that it would be at a funeral for your whole family."

"I know." Teddy embraced his cousin Hunter. "Been a long time."

"Since I've seen you, yes, but we talk all the time."

"I'm just glad you're here man." Teddy told him. It was taking everything in him to survive this day. His cousin Hunter Lewis had come and Matthew was running around being the unofficial host of the funeral.

He'd told Chase not to attend because he didn't want things to be awkward for him and for Nikki's family. Plus, the police were in attendance as well surveillancing the funeral attendees.

As Teddy continued shaking everyone's hands and receiving hugs, he was thankful that the day was almost over. It had almost been his undoing to see all the caskets sitting at the front of the church like that. He'd been counting down to the time the minister said "Amen." He was ready to begin the process of rebuilding his life and there was no time like the present to get that done.

Chapter 11

●●●

Tears fell onto the newspaper. Teddy was devestated. Seeing those three caskets at the funeral parlor that day he knew that was a day he would never forget. The imagery was so strong. His mind couldn't comprehend what had gone wrong.

He had been avoiding Chase for the last month. He hadn't spoken to her or seen her face to face. He didn't want to see anyone. He had to hand it to Chase though. She was persistent. She tried to call him every day. She sent text messages, emails, IM's, DM'd him... everything. He just didn't have the energy to fake around and put on a good front for her.

It's almost as if he wanted his life to end. He wasn't sure how he was going to go on without his sons. Not that he wouldn't miss Nikki too, but they had agreed to go their separate ways. Still, his legacy had died the same day she did. Now he had no one that would carry on his name and he didn't know if having another baby was anything that he would want to do again anytime soon. And for that, there was a hole in his heart.

"I gotta stop feeling sorry for myself," Teddy mumbled. *I need to work and focus on something other than me.* But even as he thought the words, he knew that today was one of the days he would not make it into the office. Today he was going to wallow in his own self-pity and they would have to find him there.

****

The morning of December 15 began just like any other morning. Theodore was preparing his coffee in his Keurig and reading the newspaper. After having to bury his entire family a few weeks prior, he no longer understood the meaning of life. He was having a hard time coping and therefore was using his work as an aphrodisiac with daily bouts of whiskey in his coffee to help him numb the pain.

Seeing Matthew's number flash across his cell phone screen Teddy allowed it to enter into voicemail. He knew that Matt was worried about him but he couldn't force himself to speak to anyone. Not just yet. He'd been ignoring him, Chase, and Hunter. He knew that the police were working on the case but so far didn't have any leads and he was beginning to lose hope in their capabilities. There had to be some sort of clue. Something that could point them to the right direction of who the killer might be.

Sitting in his refuge at the Four Seasons Hotel, Theodore was finding it impossible to bang out his interview with Anderson Cooper on his keyboard. Anderson Cooper was well respected in the journalist circle and had given Teddy the opportunity to interview him personally; something that he rarely allowed. Theodore wanted to make sure he did the story justice, because it was truly an honor. This meant the pressure was on because how he approached the story could make or break his career and he had the audacity to be drawing a blank.

Done with the coffee and drinking whiskey straight, the day wore on. Teddy was relaxing in the dark recesses of his hotel room trying to jumpstart his muse and tune out the distractions of the outside world. In his tranquil state, Teddy began to sense that he was no longer alone. Rising abruptly from the table in the dining room of the suite, he picked up his phone so he could turn on the flashlight app to get a better look around since the light switch was inconveniently on the other side of the hotel room.

"Who's there?" he asked into the darkness. Flipping the light switch on after crossing the room and illuminating his area with light, he saw nothing. *I'm completely bugging out,* he thought. *I've got to take my paranoia down a notch.*

Picking up his phone for the first time in a long time, Theodore decided to call Chase.

"Oh, wow. Long time, no hear stranger. How are you? You feeling ok these days?" Chase asked him with genuine concern.

"Yeah, I'm hanging in there the best way that I can. No new news."

"I know it's gotta' be hard for you. I'm always here if you ever need me just to listen. I have no problem just listening, babe."

"Do you think you could come by?" Teddy asked.

"Of course I can. Whatever you need. You know I got you," Chase told him.

"Great. I'm at the Four Seasons. Penthouse suite. I just need some company for a little while."

"I'm actually down around that way," Chase told him, "so I shouldn't be too long."

"Alright, see you when you get here." Theodore told her before disconnecting the call.

No more than five minutes later Chase was knocking on the penthouse suite of the Four Seasons.

Teddy open the door and kissed her on the cheek. "Wow, you weren't kidding. You really were right down the street." He moves to the side to let her enter.

"I told you. It's not a game," Chase said. "I'll be all over the place. You never know where I'm going to turn up." Placing her purse on the table she quickly envelope him in a hug.

"But I don't want to talk about me, honey. How are you? Seriously? It's been well over a month. I just want to make sure that you're coping with this thing and not staying stagnant because stagnation can depress you and send you into a downward spiral. And we really don't want that to happen to you."

"I know," Teddy told her as he returned her embrace. It felt good to press up on a woman's body. It had been so long since he had been this close to her.

"This whole grieving process is new to me. I'm coping the best way I know how."

"That's understandable," Chase told him. "But you got to let people in. We all want to help you and we can't help if you're staying secluded. Whatever you need I'm here," she lightly chastised him.

"I know. I promise to do better in the future. Right now I just want to spend some time with you just to get my mind off things."

Chase laughed softly, "Don't be using me just to get your mind off of things."

Teddy smiled. "You just ask what I needed."

She laughed some more. "Okay, okay, you got me there. I'm at your service Mr. Scott."

"Mmmhmmn. I think I like the sound of that," he told her as his body began to respond.

"Well, aren't you the lucky one. Ironically, I'm dressed for exactly what you need," Chase said as she removed her coat to reveal nothing underneath.

"Today must be my lucky day," Teddy replied taking in Chase's lack of dress.

"Every day is your lucky day if you choose to call me." She winked at him. "Where do you want it? Right here or you hiding a bed from me?"

"Right here is good," Teddy told her.

"Right here it is," she whispered as she tugged on the drawstring of his sweat pants. I bet that Mr. Theodore Scott needs a relief of sorts."

"I believe that you are right," Theodore replied as he allowed Chase to push his pants down and put her mouth to work on his male member.

That was the beginning of an amazing night for them. They began by the door, Teddy had Chase fur dining on the dining room table, and eventually they had made it to the bed. Teddy felt as if the weight of his shoulders had been lifted. He felt much better after releasing a few times and he had Chase to thank for that.

"You sleepy?" he asked her as she cuddled next to him.

"Mmhmmmn. A little bit," she mumbled.

"Me thinks you may have worn yourself out," he smiled.

"Me thinks you are right," Chase whispered.

****

As Theodore slept, Chase crept out of the bed. Searching around the room, she picked up her coat and left the room making sure to slide the hotel key into her pocket.

Passing through the lobby, she made it a point to say goodbye to the doorman.

Walking about a block or two away, she retrieved the duffle bag that she had hidden under a bush. Pulling out a black bob wig she quickly put it on. She reached into the bag and put on panties, a bra, a black t-shirt, black yoga pants, and black sneakers. She took off the coat she had worn to see Teddy and put on a black hoodie. Then she tucked the coat that she had previously had on into the duffle bag. After removing the hotel key, she shoved the duffle bag back under the bush.

She enjoyed a chilled walk back to the Four Seasons and entered through one of the side doors by the basement. She'd made quick work of getting rid of the cameras earlier. That's why she'd been so close when Teddy called. She wondered if he had ESP and sensed her subconsciously. Either way it had all worked out.

She makes it a point to take the back stairs. Chase knew that the workers rarely went this way during these hours so she was safe.

Letting herself back into his hotel room she quietly shut the door and put the key back where she got it from. Checking on Teddy to make sure he was still asleep, she put her plan in motion.

How dare he make me get on my knees and service him in this hotel room. Who does he think he, is degrading me like this? I will not have it. I will not. My father made me a victim once and I refuse to be a victim again, Chase thought as she pulled a knife from her bag and walked over to a sleeping Teddy.

Getting on the bed, she straddled him, smiling as he snuggled deeply into the bed. Men are all the same. Give them a little some and they down for the count.

Kissing Teddy on the cheek, she raised the knife and there was one quick swoop from ear to ear on his neck. The wound resembled a smile and rejected the smile of joy on Chase's face as the blood oozed down.

Oh, I love it, she thought. Blood excited her.

Moving quickly, she jumped off of Teddy onto the floor. She'd been careful not to get blood splatter on herself. She did a quick cleaning of the room. Not too much but just enough. She wrapped Teddy's head and throat in a plastic bag so that the bag could catch the access blood. She placed a garment bag on the floor then rolled Teddy's body into it. Hand of his body fit. She would worry about the rest in a moment. Changing the linen on the bed that she had pulled earlier that day from a maid cart, she put the soiled sheets in the garbage bag with Teddy. After making sure everything was just right, she collected all of Teddy's things and put them on the bed. Grabbing another garment bag, she overlapped it over the part of Teddy's body that could still be seen. Putting his belongings on top of the garment bag, she lent her critical eye around the room one more time before deciding she could leave. Picking up his cell phone off the table, she turned it over and took the battery and SIM card out. She didn't want anyone reaching his phone. That could turn out to be a serious tragedy.

Keeping her wig intact, she quickly removed her clothing and put on the bellman uniform that she had "borrowed." Placing her clothes in one of the garment bags that housed Teddy's body, she began her descent to the first floor and out of the hotel.

Now to dispose of this body...

Chapter 12

•••

"I haven't heard from Teddy. I'm beginning to get worried," Chase told Marcie as they sat at her house drinking wine getting ready to watch *Snapped*.

"I thought he was headed into a downward spiral after you know what happened to his family."

"Yeah. but he had texted me recently, you know. to say that he was okay and he was trying to deal with everything slowly. I don't know something seems different. This time there has been no responses at all."

"What do you think? You want to go stop by his place to see what's going on? Or you just want to wait it out some more?"

"I'm not sure. I really hadn't thought that far. I am just trying to give him his space and do the best I can with that. But you know people who go through such a traumatic experience such as that, you never know they might try to kill themselves. You don't know what's going on in their brain."

"This is true," Marcie said. "So I repeat, do you want to go over there or give it more time?"

"I think we should just give him more time just to see what happens. I don't want to crowd his space. If I haven't heard from him by tomorrow, we will definitely do a drop by just to make sure he's okay."

"Okay, sounds like a plan to me." Marcie paused. "Have you checked on Anthony at all?"

"Yes, but what I'm not too long ago he seems to be okay. He still talking that stuff trying to get back with me but I'm not really be here for that some like miss me but all this drama because I'm really I really don't care.

"Yeah, I can see that." Marcie picked up her wine glass and swirl the wine in the glass. "Thank you so much for not hating me for almost killing Anthony. It was definitely not my intention to hurt him. I had no idea."

"I don't blame you for that," Chase told her. "I blame him. You're not supposed to break into someone's house just because you want to talk to them about their best friend. Like who does that? I bet he will never do that again and his life after what happened. I feel as if he learned a valuable lesson that day and I'm thankful as well that you didn't kill him by mistake. He will never underestimate you ever going to his life believe that," Chase laughed.

"Oh, you better believe it." Marcie smile. "I am NOT to be played with. Hopefully he'll tell his friends."

"You are so dag on crazy girl." Chase laughed.

"I'm just saying. You can break into my house if you want to, your ass will end up in the hospital or the morgue."

"Can't be mad at it. They going to learn something today," Chase smirked. "But seriously I'm glad he's okay though."

"Yeah, me too. Because a shorty can't be going to jail on a murder charge."

Chase laughed out loud. "You sure can't cause nothing about that is sexy honey. I mean, I would come visit you though. I'm just saying, what are friends for?"

"Mmmhmmn, I hear you talking girl," Marcie told her.

"So, what do you make of this whole situation with Teddy and his family?" Marcie asked Chase.

Chase took a sip of her wine. "I'm not really sure what to make of it. It just seems very suspicious like someone is targeting their family."

"I know right," Marcie exclaimed. "I feel like we're in like this weird episode of our favorite show and it's going to turn out to be like some crazy neurotic chick from his past that has come back and mad at him because he didn't give her the future that she wanted."

Chase laughed. "I swear, Marce. You and your dramatics."

"I'm just saying the whole thing just seems fishy as hell. Like I wonder what he was doing before he met you, you know. Did he have a stalker? Was he stepping out on his wife prior to you? I mean it's just like we need to know these things. What if you become a target or something?" Marcie eyed Chase.

"Okay, first of all let me clear this. He did not step out on his wife with me. His wife announced to him that she wanted a divorce but she was seeing someone else, whom I think is Anthony. By the way. But that's just between you and me and he decided that he was going to start dating because she had moved on. They were separated. On their way to a divorce. That is not stepping out on your wife," Chase informed her.

"Yeah, okay. You keep telling yourself that. A married man is a married man, Chase. If he wants to get with you, he needs to wait until the divorce papers are signed and sealed. Then, and only then, is he single and that's just how I feel about it."

"So, are you saying you felt some kind of way about me and Teddy dating?" Chase needed to know.

"I don't want to seem like I'm judging you because I'm not. I'm just saying if it were me I would have waited. And back up, why do you think Anthony was dating Nikki?" Marcie inquired.

"Because he said something along the lines of his girlfriend going back to her husband and getting pregnant by him and some other stuff. I just figured that it was ironic that right around the same time Nikki pops up and tells me she's pregnant by Teddy and all that drama. It just seems very coincidental. The world is big and all but it ain't that big."

Marcie made a face. "That is just nasty. Gross. This world is way too small. I'm going to have to get my man off of an island or something," she laughed.

"Good luck with that girl. Don't you think you need to visit some islands to make that happen? You haven't had a man in years," Chase pointed out.

"But who's keeping track, right?" Marcie's voice became serious. "I feel like you sit over there on your pedestal judging mean when you're the one that was dating a married man. At least I can keep my stuff to myself until I find a guy who's worth my time and attention and not one that I would have to share with someone else."

"You take that back right now." Chase put down her wine glass.

"I'm not taking anything back. You're acting all high and mighty and your situation isn't really better than my situation. What do you expect to happen with Teddy if Nikki hadn't met an unfortunate death? She wasn't divorcing him no time soon you could tell especially with the baby coming. Which, by the way, did he ever explain that whole situation to you? Where the baby come from? She wasn't leaving her husband anytime soon. So you tell me what is it exactly that you thought you were doing?"

"Well, it's nice to see how you really feel," Chase told her. "You've been harboring all of these negative thoughts about me. I thought we were friends."

"I am your friend. That's why I'm telling you about yourself. And the only reason we even got to this point is because you don't know what to say out of your mouth about me. Let me handle my affairs the way I handle them and you handle yours the way you handle them. There's no judgement here but don't sit there and think you're better than me just because I've been single until I find somebody that I really want to spend my time with. There's nothing wrong with that," Marcie told her. "It's actually better to be that way. It guarantees that I don't have to deal with the stupid ignorant things that you have to deal with."

"I'm not really feeling you right now. I'm not feeling this conversation I think I don't want to be bothered."

Marcie put placed her wine glass on the table. "I think it's a very convenient for you. You're known to feel as if you can say what you want to say but when someone does the same to you all of a sudden, you don't want to hear it and you don't want to be bothered. You're such a hypocrite and you really need to get it together."

"Whatever, Marcie," Chase told her no longer in the mood. "I'm not this bad person that you make me out to be."

"I never said you were a bad person, Chase. That's your own insecurities. I don't think you're a bad person. I'm just asking you to cut me some slack. Your situation isn't all peaches and roses over there. That's all I'm saying. Neither is mine but I don't make any comments about your life so leave me to my life.

"Fair enough. I'll leave you to yours and you leave me to mine," Chase stated.

"That is fair," Marcie told her. "And come give me a hug. I don't want there to be any awkward tension between us."

"I don't want to hug you. I don't know if I like you right now." Chase told her cutting her eyes away from Marcie.

"You'll be okay. Come on, come give me a hug." Marcie sat up, walked over to Chase, and laughed.

Chase couldn't help but to start laughing, too. "You are such a clown."

"I may be a clown, but you love me." Marcie told her as she kissed her on the cheek before standing up to retrieve her wine glass and reposition herself on the sofa so that they could settle in for an evening of *Snapped.*

****

Anthony watched them in the distance. He saw them have a heated argument and then hug it out. *Women could do things like that,* he thought, *and still be cool.* He'd come hoping for a moment with Chase, but with Marcie there he was going to have to wait until another day. He wasn't looking forward to another encounter with Jack the Ripper at the moment. He'd barely survived their last encounter together.

Chapter 13

● ● ●

Anthony felt as if he were owed something after Marcie attacked him at her place. He felt as if she and Chase should be at his beck and call.

He had almost lost his life that fatal day he showed up at Marcie's house hoping to get more information about Chase and the guy that she called patty. He had never anticipated her attacking him with the kitchen knife and him almost losing his life ending up in the hospital praying for God to save him.

So as he has a bouquet of flowers pink carnation because they were her favorite he hoped that she would give him the benefit of the doubt all he has to endure. He knocked and waited.

Chase opened the door surprised.

"Hey what are you doing here?"

"I came by to see you," Anthony told her.

"I wish you would have called first I have other plans today."

"I just wanted to stop by for a moment to see if I can talk to you."

Chase sighed. She could at least listen to what he had to say.

Moving to the side as he entered her home she took the carnations from him as he handed them to her. Following behind him, she pointed for him to sit on the sofa and she sat in the chair across from him.

"What's on your mind, Tony?" She asks him hoping he would just go ahead and get to the point.

"I've been doing some real soul searching, you know, ever since the incident at Marcie's house and I want to make things right with you."

Chase remain silent just observing him.

"I know I should have been at Marcie's that day but I just wanted to get her perspective. If she thought that I had another chance with you or not."

She just shook her head. "Well, you have Marcie's number. Why didn't call her? Why would you break into her home attempting to talk to her about me? That doesn't even make sense, Anthony, and you know it doesn't make sense. That sounds crazy. Part of me thinks you're going to do something and she just got to you first. And that's all I see is she strikes first, ask questions later." Chase drug you just got caught up in the mix.

"I wasn't trying to do anything, seriously. I just wanted to talk to her about you."

"Why are you talking to anyone about me, anyway? If you want to know something, you know you can always come talk to me."

"Yeah, but you haven't been feeling me lately and you've been acting like you don't want to talk to me every time I try to reach out so I try to go another route."

"Oh yeah," Chase asked, "and how did that work out for you?"

Anthony was beginning to think it was a bad idea to stop by Chase's house. She was going out of her way to be an asshole and he really wasn't feeling her at the moment.

"Maybe this wasn't a good idea." He said. "I really did want to talk to you about the potential of there being an 'us' but I see that's not where you're at so maybe it's better if I just leave." He stood.

Chase stood as well. "Thanks for the flowers. I really do appreciate you stopping by. But next time if you could call first that would be great. Thanks."

"Yeah, whatever," Anthony said with much attitude. "If I choose to talk to you again, I'll call first. Later," he said as he walked out the door.

****

"I'm confused as to why I'm here."

Chase was visibly irritated. Not too long after Anthony has left, the police showed up and knocked on her door asking her to come down to the station for questioning about the death of Nikki and her children and the disappearance of Teddy. As if she didn't have enough on her plate already now she had to deal with this.

I want to have some sex with you.

Chase road her eyes slightly as she sat in the chair and the interrogation room.

"In my other ride?"

"No," the officer told her. "Like I said, we're just trying to get some facts from you to understand what was going on and your role, if there is a role to be had."

I swear this is bullshit, Chase thought to herself.

"Fine. Since you have me here, what is it that you want to know?" She knew she had attitude but she didn't care. They were really getting on her nerves today. And she had enough going on in her life, she didn't need this too.

"Where were you on the night Nikki Scott was murdered?"

"What do you mean, where was I? I was at home. My girl Marcie was there with me as well."

"And that's all that's all you have to say? That's why I love as you are and Marcie were at your house." The officer gazed at her as if she weren't telling the whole truth.

"That's exactly where I was and you can call her as well and she will verify that. We were sitting at home drinking wine talking about the no good men in our lives if you must know. Anything else?" she asked with an attitude. She was trying very hard to

MY BOYFRIEND'S WIFE 2

be respectful to the police officer but she knew her temper would take over shortly.

"Actually, there is something else I would like to know," the officer began.

"You know what, unless you're asking me I have nothing left to say," Chase told the officer. "I'm done with this. May I be escorted out? I would like to go home now."

The officer stared at her a long time before responding.

Chase could tell she had put the officer off with her attitude but she really didn't care. She didn't understand how they had the right to bring her down here to question her in the first place.

"You're free to go," the officer told her as he stood up and waited for her to leave the room.

"Great," Chase told him as she bounded out the room. She didn't have time for this nonsense. She had a job to do.

****

"Can you believe they had the nerve to bring me in for questioning?" Chase asked Marcie as she was driving home.

"Bish, what? Why?" Marcie exclaimed.

"They were questioning me about Teddy's wife's murder. Can you believe that? As if I would do anything to mess with her kids and her pregnancy and all of that. Like really? That's the best they could do? I told them I had nothing to do with that and that you and I were at my house that night drinking wine and talking about the no good men in our lives. Then I politely told them that I was ready to go and unless they were arresting me I will be answering no more questions."

Marcie began laughing. "Now that is crazy. So, does that mean they're going to be calling you now?"

"I'm not entirely sure," Chase told her. "But I mean at least now you have a heads up that they probably will because they're snooping around I guess trying to figure out what's going on because they have no other leads to work with."

"Well this is definitely good to know. Not exactly how I wanted to start my day but OK," Marcie told her.

"Yeah, I feel you on that. I'm really not in the mood for none of this nonsense today. I'm really not. I wish everybody would just get it together and keep it pushin', seriously."

"I'd say don't sweat it. We have bigger things to worry about right now. Like you're supposed to have an interview in an hour in the city. Where are you?" Marcie quickly switched into agent mode.

"I know. I'm on my way to the studio now. Traffic is a little crazy. I may be a little late but I'm coming."

"No, you cannot be late. You're going to be on *Kelly and Michael* live today. You're going to have to get it together. They don't wait and when you can, I'll be late for this Chase. I'm sorry that the police had you stuck at the station but you're going to have to figure something out. I need you to be on time. It's a bad reflection on both of us," Marcie told her.

"I mean, what you want me to do fly?" Chase responded with a hint of attitude in her voice. "I'm doing the best I can. It wasn't my intention to be late; I had no idea the cops were going to bring me in."

"Okay, fine. We'll just see you when you get here." Marcie disconnected the call.

She shook her head as she rolled her eyes wondering how their pleasant conversation had ended on this note. *She loves me like a sister but when she got into work mode sometimes, she could be real demanding and not understanding.* Chase sighed as she prayed traffic would break so she could get to the station on time and save face for Marcie and herself.

"You made it!" Marcie exclaimed a short while later.

"Of course, I made it. Don't I always? You know that I am not going to let you down," Chase informed her.

"I know," Marcie smiled, "but you've had so much on your plate lately that I haven't been entirely sure if everything was going to work out. And we all know how this New York traffic can be. You can have all of the good intentions in the world and things can still go off course."

"Don't I know it," Chase laughed. "Did I make it in time to still get hair and make-up done?" she asked.

"Barely, but they are going to have to work it out for you."

"Yes, honey. Because I need someone who is really going to beat this face to capacity," Chase emphasized.

"They are professionals. Trust and believe me, they got you covered," Marcie told Chase as she escorted her to her dressing room to get ready.

"Hey Marce," Chase called her as the make-up artist and hairdresser were in the process of taking her from a five to a ten. Getting her completely glamorized. "I want to apologize about the other night. It was never my intention to be a jerk to you and act the way I acted. While it was difficult listening to many of the things you said, the truth is that I needed to hear them."

"Mami, you know that it is no problem. Ever. I love you regardless. I think our emotions were just running high from the past events that we've been dealing with lately is all. Now, no more about it. Think about what you're going to say out there and get ready for an amazing interview," Marcie encouraged.

"Thanks, Marce. I will. You're the best friend and agent ever."

"I know this, boo." Marcie winked at her as she made her way to the stage where the interview was to take place.

Chapter 14

●●●

"Hey baby, we got to take a trip," Hunter told Lorna.

"What's going on?" Lorna asked him.

"My cousin Teddy has gone missing. I haven't heard from him in a few weeks, which isn't like him at all. You know we usually talk every day."

"I know you do. I didn't realize it had been so long. Why didn't you say anything before now?" Lorna asked.

"Because at first I thought he may have been on assignment and just been busy, but now that it's been about 3 weeks that seems highly unlikely. You know he would have called or come by now."

Lorna nodded her head. "You're absolutely right. I'm so sorry. So what time do we need to be ready?"

"We need to be ready soon. Have the nanny come so she can watch the kids. I don't know how long we're going to be gone so we just need to prepare ourselves for the worst."

"You got it, honey," Lorna told him.

Hunter paced the office back and forth. Things had changed too much for him since his beloved Ananda had passed away and he and Lorna had taken all the children in. Their home stayed booming with noise at the children played all over.

Lorna was no longer his assistant. He had done the right thing by her and married her. She had held him down from day one and refused to go anywhere. People like that you just don't give up on. You reward them for holding things down even when you didn't deserve for them to. Hunter had made it a point to love her as much as he could. But he knew deep down that Lorna was no fool. She knew that underneath it all that Ananda would always be his one true love. And trying to live up to the memory of someone was the hardest thing to do. She felt like she was always in a competition with a ghost and the ghost always won.

Not that she wanted an award or anything, but a little recognition would go a long way. She had taken on four children just to be with him. And when she had broached the subject of having a baby of her own with him he has seemed uninterested. Which didn't help the situation and her pain because now the living ghost had his baby over top of her as well. It just wasn't fair. She wanted something tangible to latch him to her forever and he refused to give in. She hated to it that but a part of her was becoming resentful of the whole situation. Just like this new thing with his cousin, it seems like another excuse do not deal with the issues that they had in their own house. He would rather go across town and deal with whatever his cousin had going on over there. And Lorna loved him. She did to the moon and back. But how much was one's body supposed to be able to take? It just wasn't fair and she was getting tired of fighting a battle that two people needed to fight.

Glancing at the hall mirror, she noticed the circles around her eyes. She missed her sexy vixen days. These days she resembled more of a housewife with her hair all over her head. She didn't have time to get herself together. She felt like a soccer mom. She used to have time to get her nails done, get her hair done, and keep her face beat. But going from a mother of zero to a mother of four in a matter of a few weeks can take a toll on anybody. And she was tired. All of them rarely did anything together and she was actually surprised that he wanted her to come with him to find his cousin

Teddy. This is the first thing they would be doing together in a while. And truth be told, she wasn't that excited about any of it.

****

"I feel weird about leaving the kids like this," Lorna told Hunter while they were in his car making their way towards Teddy's house.

"They'll be okay. We need some time alone anyway."

Lorna rolled her eyes. She didn't see how going to check on his cousin served as quality time for the two of them. But, whatever. She had learned the hard way. It was Hunter's world. Whatever he wanted or said is what it was and everyone and everything else had to fall in line.

She wished she hadn't been so stuck on him because then she wouldn't be in this mess now.

Gazing longingly out the websites, she prayed for another life in another world. One where Ananda had never existed. Then maybe she and

Hunter could have had a chance in this one. Now she would never know.

****

Hunter and Lorna entered Teddy's apartment and to their surprise, everything appeared normal.

The newspapers were stacked in a bin by the door where Teddy liked to keep them. Hunter bent down to see the date on the newspaper and it had the current date.

The apartment smelled of coffee and Pine Sol as if someone had just made a fresh cup then cleaned. Nothing was out of place.

Hunter wrinkled his forehead. He couldn't understand. If Teddy was good, why hasn't he heard from him in the past few weeks?

"Something about this place doesn't feel right," Hunter told Lorna.

"Why do you say that?" Lorna asked him. "Everything seems normal. You can tell someone is living here. Maybe he just doesn't want to talk to you right now. With the death of Nikki and everything he may just be going through a lot," Lorna said, doing her best to reassure Hunter.

"But that's what I mean. It's almost too perfect in here. As if someone is going out of their way to make it seem like everything is normal, even though it's not normal. Does that make sense?" He looked at her inquisitively.

Lorna didn't know what to say so she remained silent. Obviously Hunter was hell-bent on believing something happened to his cousin, so she was just going to be there as a supportive little wife.

"Okay, baby. Tell me what it is that you would like for me to do. Do you want me to look through something do you want me to research something? Like, tell me what it is that you need from me?"

"Right now I just want us to search his place. It's been years since I've been here so I don't know if something is out of place. But let's just see if we can find anything. Any clues that we could take to the police."

"You got it honey. Anything you need. I'm going to start with the bedroom, okay babe?" Lorna asked him.

"Yep, starting with the bedroom is a good choice. I'm a walk around his office and see if he was working on anything out of the ordinary or if I can see anything that was going on."

"Okay, sounds like a plan." Lorna told him. "Teamwork makes the dream work. Let's do this. Break." She clapped pretending they were in a huddle.

Hunter laughed. Sometimes his wife could be pure comedy. Don't get him wrong, she was no Ananda, but she came in a close second. She'd managed to do what no other woman on earth had by getting him to propose to her and then go through with the marriage.

As Hunter glanced around Teddy's office, he thought about him and Lorna's last argument over children. She wanted a baby badly but Hunter was no fool. He didn't run a successful company by being a fool. Lorna wanted a baby to be able to be tied to him forever. And even though they were married, he wasn't sure if he was ready for that type of commitment. They already had four children in the house one of which was biologically his. He couldn't seem to justify having another baby this soon, and he needed Lorna to understand that before he demoted her status from wife to mere nanny.

"Babe everything back here looks good," Lorna yelled out from the bedroom. "Nothing seems to be out of place, even though I wouldn't know if there was any way since I don't live here," she couldn't help throwing in for good measure.

"Yeah I'm with you on that one. His office looks like he's been working out of it consistently. He has a brand new interview that it seems like he's working on that he just did last week. So maybe I'm bugging out for no reason. I do want to talk to his girlfriend though and see if she's spoken with him or knows anything."

"Girlfriend? What girlfriend? You never mentioned anything about that to me," Lorna accused him.

Hunter sighed. "Lorna, I don't have to tell you everything that's going on with my family. It wasn't my business to tell you. Plain and simple. He's still married to Nikki so I didn't mention it until he figured out what he was going to do."

"What do you mean your family?" Lorna asked ignoring the rest of his statement. "Aren't I also your family? I'm confused by what it is you're trying to say."

"That's not what I meant. Don't take it like that. You always have a habit of becoming a victim and taking things too personally."

"So not only am I selective family. Now I'm a victim because I take things too personally. I swear you are a piece of work." Lorna shook her finger at him. "I don't need this. I'll be waiting for you in the car. You can search your "family's" place by yourself and try to figure it out. I'm done." She marched past Hunter and out the door.

Hunter took a deep breath. One thing he was not in the mood for was Lorna's attitude today. This is one of the disadvantages of promoting an assistant into a wife. He had definitely learned from his mistake and if things didn't get it together back to an assistant or nanny, she would go. He honestly didn't need the theatrics in his life. All he wanted was peace. Someone who did what he told them to do without all the back talk. That's it. Nothing more, nothing less.

Chapter 15

● ● ●

Chase was surprised when she arrived home to find a distinguished looking gentleman and alluring lady waiting on her doorstep for her.

"Hello, how may I help you?" Chase asked them suspiciously.

Hunter stuck out his hand. "Hi, you must be Chase. I'm Theodore Scott's cousin Hunter Lewis. He has spoken very fondly of you."

Chase responded thoughtfully as she returned the handshake.

"Yes, I am Chase. And I'm sorry he has never mentioned you to me." She waved her hand past her face. "But that's neither here nor there. What can I do for you?" she asked sweetly.

"May we come in?" Hunter asked.

Chase groaned inwardly. She hadn't planned on company. Whether it be Teddy's cousin or not. She wasn't necessarily in the mood today or any day for that matter to entertain his relatives.

"Sure," she told him as she fished through her purse for her house keys.

She prayed that Marcie would do her a solid and come by unannounced today so that she wouldn't have to be alone with Teddy's family for too long.

"Come on in and have a seat." She pointed to the living room as they enter her home letting them know that she intended for them to sit on the sofa.

"Thank you so much for your hospitality," Hunter told her. "We're here today because I'm concerned about my cousin's whereabouts. I haven't been able to get in contact with him for the past few weeks and I know that he was dating you, so I'm just curious to know if you have heard from him or if he said he was going on any trips or anything. I'm just really worried about him. It's not normally his style to disappear from the face of the earth. Even his cell goes to voicemail every time I call it. which isn't the norm either. My wife Lorna and I apologize for dropping by unannounced, but we would just like to find some answers."

Chase put her purse and her workbag on the chair.

"No, Teddy didn't mention anything to me about a new assignment or going on any trips. I spoke to him a few days ago, but I'm concerned as well because I was trying to give him space after what happened with Nikki and the kids and then one day he just stops responding. I don't know. like. I haven't had that much contact with him as well and I've been so busy with work that it has been relatively easy to give him his space."

Hunter stared at Chase at a loss for words. "Well, did you think to file a missing person report?"

"No, I did not," Chase informed him with an edge to her voice. "I wasn't aware that I should."

"Well if you haven't heard from someone in a while," Hunter began, "I would think that the next course of action would be to try and locate someone in the family or just see what was going on with that person. Have you been to his place at all?"

"No, I haven't been there recently." Chase told him slightly insulted by his statement. "I didn't know that it was my job to file a missing person report especially since I don't even know if he is in fact missing," she pointedly told Hunter.

Hunter continued staring at Chase trying to figure her out. He couldn't understand why she was on the defensive. He just wanted to know if she had heard from his cousin. But he seemed to be the only concerned party in the room since Chase felt as if his cousin needed space and didn't seem too concerned.

"It's just not like Teddy to go missing for weeks on end. When is the last time you heard from him?" Hunter willed himself to remain calm and took another stab at getting information from Chase.

"You know what, this is beginning to sound too much like a police interrogation and since I just recently did that I'm not really interested in going down that road today so I would like it very much if you to left my home," Chase told him, pleasantries gone out the window. She didn't believe it to be fair for Teddy's cousin to come here and attack her like this.

Hunter appeared shocked. He couldn't understand how someone who Teddy was so into and thought was all about him didn't seem to care about his whereabouts one-way or the other. Hunter graciously stood up off the sofa and indicated for Lorna to do the same.

"We do apologize for inconveniencing you and taking up your time. If by chance you do hear from Teddy can you, please have him call me?" Hunter handed her one of his business cards. "Thanks again and we're sorry to interrupt your day," he told her as he escorted Lorna out of the home back to their waiting car.

"She seems as if she's hiding something," Lorna said once they were out of ear reach of the house.

"I agree," Hunter replied, "she's hiding something, but I don't know what or why for that matter. But I'm definitely going to make it my business to find out."

"As I think you should, darling. Something about her is just not right. I don't know what it is but she rubbed me the wrong way from the moment she saw us standing on her step. We need to find out what she knows because something tells me she knows a hell of a lot more than she's letting on. Maybe we should contact Matt to see what he knows about the situation. We haven't really heard too much from him either, which is strange because he and Teddy are like ice and water. They go together like that," Lorna laughed.

"Yeah, you're absolutely right," Hunter responded. "I completely forgot about Matthew. Let's drop by their office and just see if he knows anything about what's going on."

"Sure, let's go," Lorna said as the driver pulled off in the direction of Teddy and Matthew's office downtown.

****

"Hey fam! What y'all got going on?" Matthew's cheery voice greeted Hunter and Lorna as they entered Teddy's office.

"Nothing much," Hunter told Matthew as he shook his hand.

"What brings you to the neighborhood?" Matthew asked. "You seen Teddy?"

"No." Hunter responded. "that's what brought me and my wife down here. We just stopped by Chase's house to see if she had any information about Teddy's whereabouts but she practically kicked us out. So I thought I would stop by here to see you and get any information that I could."

"I don't think I can be any good to you," Matt told them. "I haven't spoken to Teddy's since he left town to do the Anderson Cooper interview and when he came back he told me was staying at the Four Seasons to, you know, just decompress and get the interview written up for the paper. That was the last I heard from him. I've been trying to give him space to grieve over the loss of his family. I haven't been pressing him out too much. I was going to give him about another week and then I was going to go down there and flush him out to close down a bar with me or something just to get him out the house and around people so he's not constantly thinking of missing his family."

"It seems like we were all trying to do the same thing, but in the process I do believe that he has gone missing."

"You don't think he did something to himself do you?" Matt asked. "I hope he didn't commit suicide or nothing. You know, I've never seen him that depressed before. He was definitely having a hard time coping."

"Yeah, he was taking this whole ordeal pretty badly. But even in the worst of situations, Teddy isn't the type to kill himself. He may bury himself in his work for a little while, but he would never take his own life. He's much too strong for that. And at the end of the day, he will be in contact with someone. As it stands, no one has heard anything from him. That's what has me concerned." Hunter told Matt.

"When you put everything like that, you do have a point. Maybe we should file a missing person's report or something."

"I think we should. I'll actually take care of it. Thanks for taking out time to talk to me man. I appreciate it."

"Sure. Anytime Hunter, anytime. I just want our boy to be all right. I would hate for anything bad to happen to him on top of everything else that is already gone down with his family."

"My sentiments exactly. We're going to figure it out." Hunter extended his hand to Matt, "Thanks for everything."

"No, thank you for bringing everything to my attention," Matthew told Hunter as he returned the handshake. "Please keep me posted if you have any new updates."

"I'll be sure to do that. Have a great day," Hunter told him as he and Lorna exited the building.

"This whole situation is very strange," Lorna said once they were outside

"It is very strange," Hunter acknowledged "And I'm going to make sure I get to the bottom of it."

Chapter 16

● ● ●

"Don't you think maybe you should hire a private investigator for this?" Lorna asked Hunter. She was surprised at his willingness to get his hands dirty and do something himself for once. This was definitely a new development.

"Normally I would, but I don't want anyone to know that this is happening," Hunter told her.

"Apparently, Chase has something to hide and whatever I find I want to be able to be the first one to make an analysis of it."

"Sounds good to me. What is it that you need me to do to help?" Lorna asked him.

"Through my company I was able to find her birthday and her social security number so I need you to investigate and do as much digging as you can. Just tell me what you come up with those two things. Check her credit, check her bills every month, check her insurance policies, check anything you can. Just find something that I can work with and we'll go from there."

"You got it, boo. Anything you need I will make it work for you. I'll be back in a little bit. I'm going to go get my research started."

"Great," Hunter told her.

Hunter was revisiting Teddy's apartment again trying to find clues. Anything that would help him figure out what happened to his cousin. He was doing his best not to go into panic mode and he didn't want to contact the police until he was certain that Teddy was in fact missing. Matthew had a point with everything that had gone down with Nikki and the boys. Teddy really could have just faded into the background to give himself some time and space to deal with the major changes in his life and Hunter really didn't want to come in between him and his grieving process.

But on the flip side of that, he also knew his cousin and knew that at some point he would touch base trying to figure out what was going on with everyone or just to let people know that he was okay.

"Okay, come on Theodore. You gotta' help me out here. Where are you?" Hunter said staring at Teddy's photo on the bookcase. He really needed some help at the moment.

Hearing the phone ring in the distance caught Hunter's attention.

Following the sound Hunter open the closet door that was in the hallway and saw what was a duffel bag lying on the floor. Picking up the duffle bag, he opened it to notice a phone lying inside.

Grabbing the phone, he attempted to answer it before it stopped ringing but by the time he had answered the other person had hung up. Because it was a private call, he had no way of knowing who was on the other end of the phone. There was no way that he could trace it.

"Hunter Lewis here," he said into his cell phone once it began to vibrate at his hip.

"Baby, you will never guess what I found out," Lorna's excited voice came across the line.

"What you got for me?" he asked her.

"So, apparently your girl made about ten million dollars from her dad's death. Her dear father passed away not too long ago and the money was just released to her."

Hunter shrugged. "Okay. I mean ten million seems to be a lot, but what does that have to do with anything? Her dad did pass away. I had heard about that. I think Teddy did mention it not too long ago. From natural causes I believe."

"Well," Lorna continued, "what you don't know is that he had a history of molesting Chase. She was a victim of his for years. There's a whole file on it and everything. It's a sealed file but it's on there. Of course I was able to access it because I have all her information, but yes once upon a time Chase accused him of molesting her and they were able to settle it out of court. I guess her dad never did any jail time, but I wonder if that was always an issue for her. I'm sure it was. I can't imagine what that does to a person. I'm almost certain that unless she received extensive counseling that she probably never got over that. AND! Why would you take out a ten-million-dollar policy out on your dad? Which she also took out a month before his untimely death. I'm just saying it looks a little suspicious," Lorna stated. "What do you think?"

"I think that's very interesting to know. And we should definitely look into that more just to see what was going on. I find it very suspicious. But that doesn't necessarily mean she has anything to do with Teddy going missing. Unless you found an insurance policy on him as well that she took out, we have nothing to go on or nothing to show that she's part of the reason that I believe Teddy is missing."

"What I just find out is coincidental," Lorna began," because if she did something to her dad it's not too far-fetched that she would do something to Teddy as well. I'm just saying. I think we need to look very closely at the records just to see what's going on. With her being a famous writer and filmmaker and, you know, definitely in the limelight I'm thinking she may have been embarrassed about the whole Nikki situation. It makes you start to wonder how it is that Nikki and the boys died and then all of a sudden Teddy goes missing? It all just seems very coincidental and it seems to start with her. Before there was a Chase, there was never any problems. That's all I have to say," Lorna threw in.

"Now that you say all of that, it does make one begin to wonder what was really going on." Hunter began to see things from Lorna's prospective. "We'll definitely have to look more into the situation. Good job, babe. Good job."

"You know I always got you, papi. I love you."

"I know you do." Hunter told her. "I think I just may love you too."

****

Lorna came into the room with all the information that she had collected on Chase. They were back at the loft she and Hunter shared with their four kids in Tribeca, New York.

"What is all that?" Hunter asked as he pointed to all the files that Lorna was carrying in her arms.

"This, my darling, is all the information I could find on Chase," Lorna told him. "You will never believe all the crap that's in this woman's file. I don't see how she managed to become such a well-known individual and no one found out about this stuff."

"Well, if records are sealed for the most part, no one is entitled to that information but her."

"Well, your mami definitely hit the jackpot. You owe me and you owe me big. Like baby big," Lorna emphasized so that Hunter would get the point.

"That big, huh?" Hunter eased a lazy smile on his face.

"Yup. Major, huge."

"I'll be the judge of that. Tell me what you got."

"Okay." Lorna excitedly set on the floor with her legs crossed. "Firstly, Teddy's woman has major issues." Lorna looked up at Hunter, "I mean major, baby. This psychotic chick resorted to killing birds, squirrels and snakes after her father began molesting her. She did not dispose of these animals. She skinned them all first and then stuffed them to keep them as souvenirs. Her mother, Melissa, disgusted with her, sent her to counseling to try to get her some help. None of that seemed to work and it kind of got swept up under the rug."

"When she turned eighteen she accused her father of all type of sex crimes, but that was swept under the rug as well because as I told you on the phone it was settled out of court. She rarely speaks to her mother because according to her file, she resents her for not saving her when she was younger. Though the mother has always maintained that she knew nothing about what was going on. She and her father never had a relationship and then all of a sudden this year she takes out a ten million insurance policy on him and he dies a month later. With her sick pattern of behavior, she probably tortured him in the confines of his home for the majority of his senior years."

"I say all this to say who knows what type of emotional break her father's death caused her to have. The object of her rage is gone, so that tried me she probably needs a new target and wait for it." Lorna paused, "Enter Teddy and Nikki. I bet you Chase saw he was a songwriter and chose him. I bet you."

"Wow. That is a lot of soak in," Hunter told her. "I think you watch too much criminal minds," he joked.

"That's beside the point." Lorna I told him. "Whether I watch too much of it or not doesn't change facts. All that stuff makes sense now. Like, this stuff really happens to people."

"I think you should look into it," she told Hunter.

"I don't even need to look into it. I believe you. Everything about Chase is suspect. Even now, we haven't even heard from her to see whether or not she's heard from Teddy and it's been over a week now. Her lack of concern is what makes her guilty to me."

Chapter 17

• • •

Flashback

"Do you ever think about the old days?" Chase asked him. "Do you ever wish that you could go back in time and change the things that you've done?"

"No, I don't live with regrets," Terrence responded.

Chase stared at him with hatred in her eyes. "You're really going to sit here and say you have no regrets about your life? Not even one?" she asked him.

"Not one regret," he told her matter-of-factly.

"I find that interesting," Chase told him. "Even in your old age you refuse to acknowledge what you did to me and you refuse to apologize. You sit here with a straight face and nothing. Nothing at all. I can't believe you. I'm very disappointed to see that you have no remorse."

Terrence stared at her with very little warmth to his face. "Chase, what do you want from me? There is no love lost in our relationship. I don't want anything from you but you obviously want something from me. What is it? Let's stop beating around the bush and just get to it."

"I want you to be sorry you self-righteous son of a bitch. Can you give me that? You owe me that."

"I don't owe you a damn thing. You make sure you hit me where it hurt. You took my life away from me. My wife is only with me because she feels sorry for me. So what else is it that I can give you?"

"You know what? Nothing. I don't know what I was hoping this lunch would accomplish. I don't. I don't know if I was trying to get rid of years of neglect, abuse, hurt, anger. I just don't know. I came here today wanting to know if me hating you all these years was justified. But it turns out it was very much so and that's a very sad thing to know."

Terrence shrugged. "Hey, we all lived our lives. We all made mistakes. I'm neither proud of mine nor justify my actions, but at this stage in my life I'm too old to care. You'll die with your burdens. I'll die with mine."

"Wow. So that's it. No 'I'm proud of you for making it in spite of my dad being an ass hole?' No 'Good job, Chase. You overcame the odds. When everyone was against you, including your mother, you took it upon yourself to get away from this house and make something of yourself and we're proud of you for that?'" Tears formed in Chase's eyes. "I mean that's too much to ask for, huh?"

"Yes. I do think it's way too much to ask for."

Chase narrowed her eyes. She was angry. She had hoped this lunch would help their relationship but now she could see that was no relationship to be had. Her father refused to deal with the old emails that he had pushed on her and even as an adult with their sickened history. She still wanted the approval of her father. How messed up could she be?

"You ruined my life, you know that? Everything that was good in me died those years that you took advantage of me. And even as an adult you refuse to let me find my happiness. You refuse to give myself back to me. Why? Why not be a man and own what you did? Why not be a man and apologize? Why not just stand up and say 'hey, I'm sorry I was not the dad that I should have been but I'm ready to make amends I'm ready to be that father for you I hope you forgive me for all the wrong that I've done to you.' Why can't you do that?" Chase's voice began to raise. "A father should love his daughter.

Not the way you loved me, but in a normal way. You stole that from me and as a result, I haven't been able to have a normal relationship with anyone. Anyone. I blame you for that."

Terrance picked an imaginary piece of lint off his sweater. He wasn't in the mood for Chase's dramatics today.

"Look Chase, I didn't have anything to say to you years ago about the situation. I have nothing to say to you about now. What's done is done. Let's move on."

"Maybe you can move on because it didn't happen to you but I'm stuck in the time frame of being ten years old. I'm stuck in that moment. I can't move on."

"Well that's a situation you and yourself need to work out, but as for me I'm done with this and if you can't get over it I'm done with you too. Let's just agree to disagree and we just won't be in each other's life. I'm okay with that."

"What a sorry excuse for a father you are. Unfortunately, my mother didn't know better. But who can plan for the man that you father their kids with will turn out to be a disgusting molester. You really just go into it hoping for the best. Hoping that you found the best partner to help you parent your kids in the right way. Unfortunately, everything about you was the wrong way and I'm sorry I was ever born into this family."

"I'm sorry, too," Terrence told her. "Are we done here?" he asked her.

Pulling the papers off the table and putting them into her bag, Chase stood. She had had enough. She'd gotten what she came here for. Minus the apology. But the apology had been the most important thing. The apology was needed to save a life and he couldn't give it. "Yes, we're done here," Chase told him. "That's nothing left to discuss. I hope that you have a very nice life. Actually, that's a lie. I hope you burn in hell for everything that you did to me. Your refusal to even apologize or acknowledge that you did anything to me is appalling. So burn in hell, papi. Burn in hell for all eternity."

"Oh, don't you worry my little sunshine. I've been in hell for a very long time. I'm just sad that I can't take you with me," Terrence told her with a sick grin on his face, "Although there wasn't a lack of trying. I'm still the first one that got to taste your juices."

"You nasty son of a bitch!" Chase yelled as she picked up the plate of food on the table and threw it at Terrence's head. "I hate you so much," she said as she picked up her glass cup and hit him over the head with it. "Now try that on for size." she told him as she stormed out of the restaurant determined to do what she had planned to do all along since he was unable to convince her to do otherwise.

****

He will burn in hell. I will kill him and I will enjoy it. It has all begun. I don't need a father. I never needed one. He is a dirty old man and I am going to take him out. He was never a father. He doesn't know what a father is. He has no idea about the sacrifice and the heartache it takes to raise a child.

I'm on a one-week countdown. Chase marked her calendar for a week in advance. *Terrance will die today.* She wrote on the calendar. She circled the day in red ink.

Yes. This makes me happy. The happiest I've been in a long time. Nothing like a little antifreeze to mix in a drink and make it taste better. She smiled.

Walking over to the mirror Chase began practicing facial expressions for when she learned of her father's death in a week.

I don't think I can force a tear even if I wanted to, she thought. I'm not that great of an actress. *But I can look sad,* she thought, *if I practice frowning in the mirror.* Finally, she settled on one frown that she thought was the best. This is the one. She smiled. I can tell that this is going to be an amazing week.

Chapter 18

• • •

Chase remembered it all like it happened yesterday. One day she was a girl and then the next day she turned into a full-fledged woman. All thanks to her no good "father" and she used the term very loosely.

She remembered all too vividly the day the world changed. And she held on to that day because if the last day she felt like a child. Is the last day she was running around carefree if the last day she knew what it was like to think the world was fair that anything was possible that you can overcome anything that the most enjoyment to be had was playing hopscotch in the street and jumping rope with her friends. If the day all of that change for her if they that the world wasn't as pure the Sun didn't shine as bright rainbows were for kids. The day her innocence was taken by the one man who should have been sworn to protect it with everything in his being. The man that was supposed to be her protector and look out for her and made sure the world stayed golden, that the sun continued to bring her life that everything was like roses and lollipops. But not her. In her world, that man didn't exist and he never would.

"You are just developing much too fast," her mother stated. "Just yesterday you were five years old now you look like a grown woman. You have tatas, you have a shape. Like, what is going on? I'm not ready for this. Where is my five-year-old little girl?"

Chase smiled. "Mommy, I'm not a little girl anymore."

"Oh you will definitely always be my little girl, pumpkin. I will love you to the end of time. In my eyes you are always be that five-year-old little girl no matter how big you get."

"I know, mama. I know." Chase smiled.

"Hi, beautiful." Her father kissed the top of her head as he entered the kitchen.

"Hi, daddy!" Chase beamed. Every bit the daddy's girl.

"What are my favorite girls in here up to?"

"I was just explaining to Chase that she is much too developed to be ten. I miss my little five-year-old girl who used to run around here. Now she's becoming a grown woman and I'm just not ready for this change," Chase's mother Melissa stated.

"She was just telling me daddy that I'm going to be her little girl forever. Which, I know I am." Chase laughed as she blew her mother kisses.

Terrance took in his daughters budding hourglass shape. He hadn't really noticed it before *until his wife pointed it out. "Well, what do you know? She does seem to be ripe for the picking." he thought.*

"Going to have to beat these boys with a stick. It may be time for me to go buy that shotgun," Terrence told them.

"Daddy, don't make a big deal. I'm only ten."

"My point exactly." Terrance stated.

Chase giggled at her dad. She had no idea what he was talking about. But he sounded plenty disturbed by it.

Later that evening when Chase was getting ready for bed her dad came in to say prayers with her.

"You came to say a prayer with me daddy?" Chase asked him.

"No, I came to give you good night kisses," he told her as he leaned down and kissed her on the mouth.

"Thanks Daddy good night."

"Not yet," her dad told her. "Want another one." This time he leaned down and kissed her deepening the kiss and sticking his tongue in her mouth.

"Ewww, gross daddy. I don't like that," Chase told him as she broke the kiss.

"Good. I'm just showing you what boys will do to you. Don't allow that unless it's me and don't tell your mother."

Chase nodded as she pulled the covers up to her chin.

That was the first night of many that her father began teaching her what boys would want to do with her and shouldn't do, resulting in him taking her virginity on her sixteenth birthday.

Chapter 19

● ● ●

"**Baby, I need you to** sit down. I have some very bad news to tell you," Lorna called Hunter at his office.

Hunter had a feeling of dread in the pit of his stomach. He had a feeling that he already knew what she was going to tell him. But he remained silent and allowed her to continue.

"So, the police just left our apartment. And they didn't come with good news, baby." Lorna took a pregnant pause. "They found Teddy's remains today. I'm so sorry. I know you really wanted to find your cousin alive. But there's nothing we can do now. Baby, I really truly am sorry. You okay?"

Hunter would be lying if he said he was in disbelief. He knew that Teddy's story wouldn't have a happy ending. His gut had told him that long ago and he had been forewarned. But still here and it come out of law and his mouth was almost too much for him to handle at the moment. He wasn't that much of an emotional guy but him and Teddy had grown up like brothers. They use to play together running in the field just doing everything that brothers do and now the one person that he considered a brother was gone.

"Baby?" Lorna probed.

"I'm sorry," Hunter whispered. "I'm here. I'm just trying to take it all in. Did they say what happened?" he asked.

"Unfortunately, they did. It turns out that someone had chopped his body up into little pieces. The biggest part of the body that they found was his torso. All those things were in a trash bag at the dump. The only good part is that his fingers were also in the same bag as the torso so they were able to get his fingerprints off and ID the body."

Hunter felt as if you have been got punched. That was no way for anyone to die. Especially Teddy. Nothing he had ever done in his life had made him deserving of a death as gruesome as this one.

"So, they're 100% sure that it's him?"

"Yes, baby," Lorna responded softly. "They're 100% sure, but they still want you to go down if you're up to it and check it out for yourself."

"I'm up to it," Hunter told her. It's not that he was a glutton for punishment but he just had to see it with his own eyes.

After IDing the body Hunter was numb all over. Everything in his spirit told him that Chase was the culprit and he was going to make sure that she went down. Dropping by the police station, he gave a full report of the incidents he believed to have taken place, Chase's background, and the way that she was acting suspiciously. He asked the police to pull cameras from the hotel and any other footage they may have had close to Teddy's apartment that might implicate Chase in his murder.

Because Hunter Lewis was such a prominent member of high society, the police jumped right on it. They weren't going to stop until they found a way to solve this case for Mr. Lewis and bring his family some justice.

Chapter 20

● ● ●

Chase's cell phone rang and she picked up because Marcie's number flashed across the screen.

"Hey, honey. What's good?" Chase spoke into the receiver.

"Girl, you have got to have several seat on this one."

"What is it?" Chase asked.

"They have found Teddy's body."

Chase was floored. "Are you serious? So does that mean he's really dead? Oh my gosh. I had no idea," Chase said attempting to sound as if she were in shock.

"Yes. It's all over the news," Marcie told her. "Have you not turned on your T.V. today? Or radio? Anything? Even if you go to the internet, you'll see it pop up. It's just pure craziness. They found his body sliced up into little pieces in garbage bags and tossed in the city dump. Can you believe that?"

"No, I can't believe that. It just seems so surreal. I can't believe that something like that would take place and I would have no inclination of what was going on."

"Well, you had said you hadn't heard from Teddy in a while, but I had no idea that something like this could happen. He didn't seem like the type of guy that had enemies or anything," Marcie stated.

"I know, right. It just seems very strange. That's the best way that I can sum it up."

"Doesn't it bother you at all?" Marcie asked. "You don't seem to be that affected by the news.

Girl, if this were my man, I'd be falling out on the phone somewhere losing my mind."

"Yes, girl! Of course I am affected," Chase exclaimed. "How can you ask me something like that? Of course I am devastated. I can't believe that I won't see him anymore. And his cousin Hunter had just come to visit my house remember I told you about that."

"Yes, I do remember that. I wonder how he feels." Marcie stated.

"I know. Knowing him, he is going to blame me for it. When he and his wife came to my house he made it very clear that he thought I had something to do with Teddy's disappearance or not being concerned with his whereabouts."

"I know but, he didn't have any evidence to back that up. I think it was just in his feelings," Marcie told her. "It's not like you had anything to do with that." Marcie stopped talking when she encountered Chase's silence. "I mean you didn't have anything to do with the right, Cha-cha?"

Chase woke up out of her daze. "Of course, I didn't have anything to do with it. What are you talking about? I was just getting to know Teddy. We really enjoyed each other's company. I would never do anything to hurt him."

Marcie thought that she sounded a little suspect as if she was trying to convince Marcie and herself at the same time that she was innocent.

"Ok. If you need anything just let me know." Chase looked up as two officers entered her office. "Ma'am sorry, you need to hang up the phone. We hate to do this at your work place, but you're under arrest."

"What is going on in your office?" Marcie asked. "Did I just hear someone say that you are under arrest?"

"Yeah, the police are here. Meet me down at the station with bail money," Chase told her as she hung up the phone.

****

"I demand to know what is going on this instance!" Marcie yelled at the police officer. "You have booked my friend unjustly and I want her released."

"Ma'am, you're going to have to have a seat and be quiet before I have to book you for disorderly conduct."

Marcie was livid. They wouldn't let her see or talk to Chase.

"You may as well go home. Your friend was booked on murder charges. She's going to be sitting for a while. There will be no bailing her out tonight."

"This makes absolutely no sense." Marcie stood at the station in disbelief.

"Whether it makes sense or not ma'am this is what it is. I advise you to go home because if you stay here any longer the likelihood of you getting booked is at 100%." the officer stated.

"There has to be a mistake."

"Ma'am, go home. You're beginning to upset me and I'm about to book you."

"Fine. I can tell when I'm not wanted." Marcie spun on her heel in anger.

Later that evening Marcie's cell phone rang. Even though it was an unknown number, she answered anyway.

"Hello."

"I heard you came down and tried to bail me out today." Chase whispered.

"Oh my gosh, Cha Cha. Are you okay? Girl you know I came down there acting up trying to see what was going on. Almost got booked myself. But what is going on? Why were you arrested? The officer that was handling me says something about murder charges. Are they trying to blame Teddy's murder on you?"

"That's exactly what they're trying to do and more than likely the charges are going to stick."

"What? I'm confused," Marcie told her.

"It is what it is, Marcie. I love you to death. Thank you for holding me down all these years. You're the only family I've ever had. You mean the world to me. But don't come back up here. I love you. Bye."

Marcie stared at the phone long after Chase had hung up.

Epilogue • • •

One year later

How are things in here?" Marcie asked her after giving her a hug.

Chase smiled at Marcie across the table. "As good as they can be, I guess."

"You look well," Marcie told her.

"You're just being nice. But thank you, I appreciate it."

"I still can't believe everything that has gone down in the last year." Marcie studied Chase. This was the first time Chase had allowed her to visit her. "What made you do it Cha Cha? The whole family?"

"I don't know. I had seen them out a few months before the funeral, they had appeared so happy, something in me just took over, and I wanted to kill that happiness. Everything was a set up. Me getting with Teddy. Having Anthony become friends with Nikki was part of the plan, though I didn't expect him to actually date her. That was the only surprise. Everything else I orchestrated. Sorry Marcie. I never had that perfect family and something in me just snapped and now their world is no more. I know how crazy that sounds, but that's how I felt and truth be told, I have no remorse. I would probably do it again."

"Wow, Cha. That is incredibly sad and it is a little crazy. I'm not going to lie to you."

"I like it in here though. Everybody has problems and many women have gone through something similar to what I have gone through. So they understand the depth of my feelings." Chase told Marcie. "So don't feel sorry for me. I'll be fine."

"As long as you're happy, mami. That's all that matters."

"I'm good. I promise. Just make sure you take time out of your schedule every once in a while to visit me."

"You already know I got you," Marcie told her as she gave her a quick hug.

****

In case you all are wondering...I got my baby FINALLY! It took some doing but in the words of Steve Urkel "I'm wearing you down, baby, I'm wearing you down." I have a wonderful baby boy named after his daddy. Turns out, I won after all. The memory of Ananda be damned.

xoxoxoxox! Lorna

mycheawrites@yahoo.com

www.mychea.com

BOOKS BY GOOD2GO AUTHORS

GOOD 2 GO FILMS PRESENTS

THE HAND I WAS DEALT- FREE WEB SERIES

NOW AVAILABLE ON YOUTUBE!

YOUTUBE.COM/SILKWHITE212

To order books, please fill out the order form below:

To order films please go to www.good2gofilms.com

Name:_____

Address:_____

City: _____ State: _____ Zip Code: _____

Phone:_____

Email:_____

Method of Payment: Check   VISA   MASTERCARD

Credit Card#:_____

Name as it appears on card: _____

Signature: _____

Item Name	Price	Qty	Amount
48 Hours to Die – Silk White	$14.99		
Business Is Business – Silk White	$14.99		
Business Is Business 2 – Silk White	$14.99		
Childhood Sweethearts – Jacob Spears	$14.99		
Flipping Numbers – Ernest Morris	$14.99		
Flipping Numbers 2 – Ernest Morris	$14.99		
He Loves Me, He Loves You Not - Mychea	$14.99		
He Loves Me, He Loves You Not 2 - Mychea	$14.99		
He Loves Me, He Loves You Not 3 - Mychea	$14.99		
He Loves Me, He Loves You Not 4 – Mychea	$14.99		
He Loves Me, He Loves You Not 5 – Mychea	$14.99		
Lost and Turned Out – Ernest Morris	$14.99		
Married To Da Streets – Silk White	$14.99		
My Besties – Asia Hill	$14.99		
My Besties 2 – Asia Hill	$14.99		
My Besties 3 – Asia Hill	$14.99		
My Boyfriend's Wife - Mychea	$14.99		
My Boyfriend's Wife 2 – Mychea	$14.99		
Never Be The Same – Silk White	$14.99		
Stranded – Silk White	$14.99		
Slumped – Jason Brent	$14.99		
Tears of a Hustler - Silk White	$14.99		
Tears of a Hustler 2 - Silk White	$14.99		
Tears of a Hustler 3 - Silk White	$14.99		
Tears of a Hustler 4- Silk White	$14.99		
Tears of a Hustler 5 – Silk White	$14.99		
Tears of a Hustler 6 – Silk White	$14.99		
The Panty Ripper - Reality Way	$14.99		
The Panty Ripper 3 – Reality Way	$14.99		

Continued on next page…..

The Teflon Queen – Silk White	$14.99		
The Teflon Queen 2 – Silk White	$14.99		
The Teflon Queen 3 – Silk White	$14.99		
The Teflon Queen 4 – Silk White	$14.99		
The Teflon Queen 5 – Silk White	$14.99		
Time Is Money - Silk White	$14.99		
Young Goonz – Reality Way	$14.99		
Subtotal:			
Tax:			
Shipping (Free) U.S. Media Mail:			
Total:			

Make Checks Payable To:
Good2Go Publishing
7311 W Glass Lane,
Laveen, AZ 85339